A SLAVE'S
SONG

Michael Edwin Q.

MICHAEL EDWIN Q.

Advantage
BOOKS

A SLAVE'S
SONG

A Slave's Song by Michael Edwin Q.
Copyright © 2019 by Michael Edwin Q.
All Rights Reserved.
ISBN: 978-1-59755-527-2

Published by: ADVANTAGE BOOKS™
Longwood, Florida, USA
www.advbookstore.com

Library of Congress Catalog Number: 2019936755
1.   Fiction:: African American - Woman
2.   Fiction: African American – Historical
3.   Social Science - Slavery

Cover Design: Alexander von Ness
Edited by: Nancy E. Sabitini

First Printing: June 2019
19 20 21 22 23 24   10 9 8 7 6 5 4 3 2 1
Printed in the United States of America

A Slave's Song

Dear Reader,

I dedicate this book to all the men and women whose names time has forgotten, who wrote the songs woven into this story. These songs were written by slaves, to slaves, and for slaves, songs of deep faith and strong hope.

As you read them, savor them for their beauty as you would fine poetry. Also, we learn from these lyrics what was in their hearts and on their minds. We learn a little more about and see a little more clearly the soul of the slave.

There are a few songs included that are not slave songs but were popular at the time. Each song was selected for its beauty and how well it complimented the story.

Though a work of fiction, it conveys a message of hope that still rings true today. I hope and pray that in some small way it brings people closer together.

If I can get people to read, think, and discuss, I feel I've succeeded. Never give up! Continue till there is no space between what you believe and who you are.

Blessings,

Michael Edwin Q.

"Slaves sing most when they are most unhappy. The songs of the slave represent the sorrow of his heart; and he is relieved by them, only as an aching heart is relieved by its tears."

Frederick Douglas

One

A Red, Red Rose

The war left the soil of the south bloodred. Can you remember the war with a clear memory, every face a story, sad stories that can break your heart and spirit? But there is one story that will restore your faith. For this reason alone, it needs telling. For just a moment, pull up a chair, rest easy, lend an ear, and for a moment let others play the hero. Listen and learn.

The end of the war was near. Though no one ever spoke of it, the South knew it was on its last leg. There were thirty *Johnny Rebs*, all that was left from a company of two hundred out of Georgia. They wandered the countryside, doing their best to avoid conflict of any kind. Over mountains and through valleys they marched, living on roots, berries, frogs, and turtles. They roamed about lost, but one thing was clear: They were far from home, most likely north in enemy territory. It was a strange land to them. The trees were bigger, mostly fir. The forests were denser than back home. It wouldn't have surprised them if they were as far north as Missouri. They'd walked long and hard enough for it to be so.

The sun hung high and hot, but the thick forest overhang shaded them. They looked more like a band of tramps than soldiers. Their boots were worn to the soles, exposing their feet. Their uniforms were torn and no longer Confederate gray but chimney black. They'd long since stopped marching in file, but wandered haphazardly, trying to be as quiet as possible. If the Yankees were out there, they needed to hear them before being heard by them.

Stepping into a clearing to stop and rest, exhausted, they fell to the ground with their backs flat to the earth and their heads resting on the rocks.

"Let's have a song; it'll lift your spirits," Captain Malory said, standing over his men. "Malachi, break out your mouth harp. Let's do these boys some good."

"But the Yankees might hear us, Captain."

"Let 'em hear! I'm tired of pussyfootin' around."

The leader, Captain Malory, was slightly older than the rest – a father figure. Years of leading men into battle had turned his hair and beard gray. His once large civilian belly was now flat as a board, and he could scrap with the best of them.

He always carried a photo of his beloved wife and two children, a boy and a girl, who probably would be slow to recognize him. It had been so many years since they had fixed eyes on one another. As well, he surely would not recognize his nearly grown children who had been small when he left.

He came from a well-to-do family, plantation owners. His father always hoped he would someday succeed him, but that was not to be. As a young man, Malory went off to university to pursue an education in music.

Music was his life. Back home, he was a music teacher and choir director at the university. Whenever morale was low, he'd get Malachi to blow his harmonica and get the men to singing. Years earlier when they first started singing together, they sounded like a flock of lost sheep. But after months under Malory's guidance, they sounded good enough to make any church choir proud.

Private Malachi Jones stood, took out his mouth harp, tapping it a few times in the palm of his hand. No one knew why he did that before playing; it was just one of those mysterious things harmonica players do.

Malachi was a dark-haired, good-looking, muscular young man. He'd been raised in the Deep South. His people, his father and mother, were landowners, a small amount of land to be precise. They were not rich, but they were far from poor and lived well. Malachi dreamed of the day he'd return to his family and their small farm.

Everybody in the company liked Malachi. He seldom spoke; but when he did, they'd all hush because it was usually something pretty good, be it a joke or some serious comment. Other than that, none of the others knew much about him. To them, he was just one of the company. As for his harmonica playing, they'd never heard better before or since. He knew how to get to them. Many were the nights he'd have them dancing around the fire. When they were down, he perked them up. On Sundays, he'd play hymns till every man felt like he'd been to church. But when he played something sorrowful, it was the best. They'd close their eyes and see faces of loved ones…wives, children, mothers and fathers. Somehow, Malachi's playing always made things better.

That day he put his lips to the harp and began playing the company's favorite, "The Battle Hymn of the Republic." Oh, I know what you're thinking: that's a Union song. But in those days, both sides loved the song, claiming it as their own. To the winner go the spoils.

They stood up. Captain Malory conducted like he was back at the university. If you close your eyes, you can still hear it. It makes the hair on the back of your neck stand on end and chills run up and down your spine.

> *Mine eyes have seen the glory of the coming of the Lord;*
> *He is trampling out the vintage where the grapes of wrath are stored;*
> *He hath loosed the fateful lighting of His terrible swift sword,*
> *His truth is marching on.*
> *Glory, glory, hallelujah! Glory, glory hallelujah!*
> *Glory, glory, hallelujah! His truth is marching on.*

When the song finished, no one said a word. They picked up their packs and trudged on, keeping off the roads. Now and then, they'd hear gunfire off in the distance. They'd steer clear, going in the opposite direction, which only made them feel more turned around and lost. With no maps, they had only the sun and the stars to guide them. The only thing they were sure of was that they were going in the wrong direction.

Later that day, when they stopped to rest again, the Captain reached into his pack, pulling out a suit of clothes, a Union soldier's uniform. It was as blue as the deep blue sea with gold stripes down the side of the pants and gold buttons on the jacket. There were sergeant stripes on the arms, and it was topped off with a Yankee cap. He tossed them to Private Malachi Jones.

"Here ya go, Jones; put these on. I need ya to scout ahead."

It wasn't a random choice. Malachi was the perfect selection for scouting detail. Not only because the uniform fit him like someone tailored it for him, but mostly it was because of one talent Malachi had that no one else in the company had. He could speak like someone from the North. You see, a Northern accent is very drab, tasteless sounding. Now a Southern accent with its long drawl sounds much more like singing than talking.

"Talk Yankee for us, Malachi," someone shouted.

He stood at attention. "Hello, I'm Private..."

"You're a sergeant, not a private," warned the Captain. "Don't forget your strips."

"Oh, yeah," he said, falling back to attention. "How do you do, sir? My name is Sergeant Malachi Jones, from the 304th infantry out of Boston, Mass. It's a pleasure to meet you."

They all howled with laughter.

"Now, ya know what to do?" the Captain asked.

"Sure do," said Malachi, holding his harmonica. "If there's Yanks up ahead, I take out my harp and blow "Always Stand on the Union Side," and I blow "Dixie," if the coast is clear."

"Right," said the Captain, giving him a salute. "Watch yourself out there, Jones."

They watched Malachi run off into the thick of the forest, his head bobbing up and down till the undergrowth engulfed him. Everyone sat back down on the ground; closing their eyes, they rested and waited.

After a time, Sergeant Hastings approached the Captain, speaking loud enough for all to hear. "Sir, Malachi's been gone a mighty long time. Don't ya think we should trudge on and look for him?"

"Let's give him a few more minutes, Sergeant."

Just then, the echo of Malachi's mouth harp seeped through the trees.

"Hush, the signal," said the Captain.

"What song is it?" Sergeant Hastings asked.

"You are tone-deaf, aren't ya?" laughed the Captain. "It's "Dixie", the all clear. Everyone grab your stuff, and let's go."

Now, "Dixie" is a grand old tune. When a brass band plays it, you can't help but want to march off to war. But Malachi always played it soft and slow, like a love song. They followed the sound till it was no longer an echo but a clear-to-the-ear sound. Hastings took hold of the Captain's sleeve to stop him from moving further.

"Captain, something's wrong. True, I may be tone-deaf, but I tell ya that ain't Malachi playing the mouth harp."

The Captain stopped, taking a good, hard listen.

"Ya know, you're right. It don't sound like him. The playin' sounds shaky. Something ain't right."

They moved forward ever so slowly and with great caution. When they got to the next clearing, they could see what was wrong. There was Malachi sitting high up in a tree, playing his mouth harp, his hands shaking like a reed in the wind. He was playing something awful. Half the notes were wrong, and the ones he hit had a sore feel to them. And it was clear why. At the bottom of the tree, standing on his hind legs, was a grizzly bear. He must have been at least eight-feet high. He growled at Malachi, showing his long, pointed teeth. He waved his paws at Malachi, his razor-sharp claws tearing away chips of bark from the tree.

"Looks like we'll have meat tonight," Hastings said as he held his rifle up, looking down the barrel at the animal.

"No, don't!" shouted the Captain. Unable to stop his instincts, Captain Malory grabbed the rifle barrel and tilted it up to the sky. The shot rang out. "Now every Yankee within ten miles will come a-runnin'," grumbled Malory.

The gun's thunderous sound took the bear by surprise. He fell down to the ground, back on all fours. He turned to growl at the small troop.

"Quick! Everyone grab a stone," Malory ordered as he bent down, picking up a large rock. The men did the same. "Aim for his face. On the count of three: one…two…three!"

They let the stones fly, most of them hitting the beast in the face and eyes. He whined, turned, and ran in fear. Malachi scurried down the tree and ran to the others.

"Let's get out of here before that beast realizes our bark is worse than our bite," said Malory.

"What about my uniform, Captain?" Malachi asked.

"Not now, no time to change clothes now. That shot's sure to attract attention. Company…double-time!"

Captain Malory ran off into the brush. The company followed. Not one had the slightest idea which direction they were going.

After some time, they began slowing down. The running became a trot, then a brisk walk, and finally a slow march. They were thirsty, hungry, and tired. Food and drink had been their biggest problems. There were times their bellies sang as loud as their voices. They'd forgotten the last time they had a real meal. They put new notches in their belts every few days.

They came up on a group of felled trees. Stuck to the underside of those trees were clusters of dark brown mushrooms. Some of the men grabbed handfuls, sniffed them, and then started to eat them.

"Hey, how do we know they ain't poison?" Private Carson asked.

Corporal Dewitt took a big bite and spoke with his mouth full. "What does it matter? Either way ya get rid of the hunger."

Later that day, they came to a stream. The men fell to their knees for a drink. Corporal Hood lay down flat and began lapping up the water like a dog.

"What in the blazes are ya doin', Hood?" Private Roland asked, pointing him out to the others.

Hood looked up. "The Lord told Gideon to lead his men to a stream. He was to keep the men who cupped their hands to get a drink and use only them in the battle. The men who drank like beasts they sent home. Well, I ain't takin' any chances. I want to go home."

"Hood, ya ain't right in the head," Roland said.

"I know that," said Hood. "I suppose the war has made *you* sane."

Roland thought about that for a moment, and then he hit the ground next to Hood and began lapping up the water.

They walked alongside the stream, following the flow. A few hours later, they came to a clearing and saw a shanty town of about a dozen dilapidated shacks. It was hard to tell if they were poorly built homes or old homes that were never kept up. Either way, they were an eyesore.

The folks who lived there came out to meet them, men, women, children, and old folks – all poor and white. They looked none too prosperous, skinny, and rundown as the sheds they lived in.

"Who's the boss around here?" Captain Malory asked.

A gray-haired fellow stepped forward. It was hard to tell how old he was; the years had not been kind.

"I am. The name's Thornton," he said. "If you're here to rob us, you're out of luck and too late. We ain't got much."

The Captain reached out, shaking Thornton's hand. "Sir, I don't know what them Yankees did to ya when they came through, but us Johnny Rebs ain't no different from you folks. We're just passing through and don't mean ya no harm."

"Let no one say that we's one to turn away a hungry Southern man without givin' him a little taste of something. We'd feel honored to have y'all as our guests," said Thornton.

In the center of this shanty town was a large one-room shack which they used as a school, warehouse, and meeting hall.

They followed the folks of the town, looking about with great caution. It was a known fact that some folks, southern or northern, sold information to whatever army was in control of the area. They did this in exchange for food or sometimes just to be left alone. They entered the main building slowly for fear it might be a trap, and all let out a sigh of relief to find no Yankees waiting to ambush them.

The soldiers sat on the floor with the men of the town as the women prepared and served them food. They heard the sound of children playing outside, which put them even more at ease.

The food was simple corn mush, but it was served with dignity, and the soldiers appreciated it as if it were a king's feast.

"Say, what's the name of this place?" Captain Malory asked Thornton.

"Ain't got no name. We just needed a place to live, so here ya are. Y'all are back in the South, ya know, but mighty close to the Northern border. This whole area is overrun with Yankees. We was all once farmhands at the local plantations and farms in this county. When the war broke out, all the young healthy men signed up. If ya look around, most of us fellers are too old to fight. What young men ya see is those that came back home after bein' wounded, too crippled to go back to war."

"Those fellers over there don't look like there's nothing wrong with 'em," Malory said, pointing across the room. "And some of those boys over there look just fine."

Thornton shook his head. "To be honest, they's deserters. Lately, some of the men who went off to war and were lucky enough to stay alive have started to return home. Anybody with any sense knows the South ain't got a snowball's chance in hell of winnin'. For us, the war is over."

"'Anybody with any sense,'" Malory repeated softly, looking sadly at his own uniform.

A large jug of corn-liquor was passed around among the men. It tasted more like kerosene and burned going down, but it warmed the heart.

Corporal Dewitt tried to strike up a conversation with one of the older men sitting next to him. "Say, old-timer, can ya see the Appalachians from here?" he asked, pointing at one of the windows.

The old man smiled, shaking his head. "Not from here ya can't; but they're not far off. I sure would like to see them just once before I die."

"Then why don't ya, old-timer?"

"I don't know. It's always something. When you're young, your father needs ya to work the land with him. Then ya get married, and ya got all these responsibilities. Then when you're older, ya ain't got no money and no strength. Not to mention famines, floods, and wars. It's always somethin'. Life has a way of interfering with your livin'."

Captain Malory stood up, walked over, and sat down next to Malachi who was still in his Yankee uniform. Malory leaned over, whispering into Malachi's ear. "I got your uniform in my pack. Ya want to change and get out of that blue getup?"

"Maybe later, I'm too plum tuckered out to even want to stand up," Malachi whispered back.

One of the townsmen pointed at Malachi. "What's ya boys doing with that filthy Yankee, anyways?"

"Heck, he's our prisoner. What did ya think?" Sergeant Hastings responded, joking.

"I don't know if I like the idea of sharin' our vittles with no filthy Yankee," said the man.

"Yeah, me too. Why don't we take him outside, find us a tall tree, get us some rope, and see if we can stretch his neck a bit?" said another man.

"Ya don't want to do that, boys," Hastings replied. "This here ain't no ordinary Yankee. He got him some special talents. That's why we keep him alive."

"Special talents…like what?"

"He can blow a mouth harp so sweet he'll make ya think ya died and went to heaven."

"Yeah, I bet."

"No, really," Hastings said. Then he turned to Malachi. "Go ahead, Malachi. Give `em a sample."

Malachi reached into his jacket, pulled out his mouth harp, and looked to Captain Malory. "What will it be, Captain?" Malachi asked.

The Captain thought for a moment. "Somethin' old and sweet, let's do 'Barbara Allen.'"

The room went silent, and all heads turned to Malachi as he played soft and sweet. After he played a full verse and chorus, the Captain looked to his men. "Come on, boys. Let's show `em what we can do."

The months of practice showed; but now with an audience, they sang like angels.

> *In Scarlet town, where I was born*
> *There was a fair maid dwellin'*
> *And every youth cried well away*
> *Her name was Barbara Allen*

> *All in the merry month of May*
> *When green buds they were swellin'*
> *Sweet William on his deathbed lay*
> *For love of Barbara Allen*

The mood was somber. Slowly, the corn-liquor jug got passed around again gently as if it were holy water from the Jordon River, used by John the Baptist himself. Miraculously, a second jug appeared.

> *He sent his servant unto her*
> *To the town where she were dwellin'*
> *O haste and come to my master, dear,*
> *If your name be Barbara Allen*

Night drew near and darkness was all around. The few lanterns with their flickering flames cast dancing shadows on the walls and ceiling. The soldiers never noticed the women of the village had cleaned up the pots and pans and all evidence of dinner. The sound of the children playing outside was no more. The women had since gathered them, washed them, made them say their prayers, and put them to bed. The hour was getting late.

> *So slowly, slowly she got up*
> *And slowly she came nigh him*
> *And the only words to him she said*
> *Young man, I think you're dyin'*

They swayed to the rhythm, their arms around one another. For the moment, there were no armies, no war, and no strangers. The world was good.

Michael Edwin Q.

He turned his face unto the wall
And death was with him dealin'
Adieu, adieu, my dear friends all
And be kind to Barbara Allen

As if on cue, the townsmen placed their arms around one another and the soldiers too. It's strange how corn-liquor can take a roomful of strangers and slowly form them into a brotherhood. They began to sway along to the slow rhythm. Then in perfect harmony...at least, to their ears it was perfect harmony...they joined in on the last three verses.

O mother, mother, make my bed
Make it soft and make it narrow
Sweet William died for me today
I'll die for him tomorrow

They buried her in the old churchyard
They buried him in the choir
And from his grave grew a red, red rose
From her grave a green briar

They grew and grew to the steeple top
Till they could grow no higher
And there they twined in a true love's knot
Red, red rose around the briar

When the last note faded, there was silence. No applause, no talking, just silence. They passed the jug around one more time. And with full stomachs, which had been empty for so long, and once-worried minds lulled by the now sweet taste of corn-liquor, each man lay down and fell fast asleep.

Two

Bound for Canaan Land

The morning sunlight barely oozed into the room. It was enough to make out shapes, but colors were still gray. Captain Malory was wakened by the muzzle of a rifle pushing against his nose. He opened his eyes and looked up to see a Yankee private smiling down on him.

"Go ahead, do somethin', anythin', so I can blow your head off." the Yankee said through grinning teeth.

Malory looked around. Armed Yankee soldiers were all around them, pointing their rifles at his sleeping men. None of the townsmen were in the room. Two of the Yankees opened the shutters on the windows. Sunlight flooded the room. The sleeping men woke, each raising their hands in surrender.

"My name is Lieutenant Gramm," shouted a gray-haired Yankee soldier standing in the doorway. "You are our prisoners. It is useless to resist. Give us no trouble, and we will treat you fairly."

Just then, Thornton walked in, standing by Lieutenant Gramm.

"Traitor!" Corporal Dewitt shouted at Thornton.

"Let `em be," Captain Malory said. "He's only tryin' to take care of his people. The Yankees are the new masters in this house. Anybody with any sense would do the same."

Lieutenant Gramm walked to the center of the room. Two rows of gold buttons ran up the front of his coat, a gold epaulette on each shoulder, his hand resting on the hilt of his saber. "Captain Honeycutt, have your men round up all their firearms and put them in the wagon."

"Yes, sir," Honeycutt snapped.

Lieutenant Gramm walked over to Malachi and smiled down on him. "Did they hurt you, boy?"

"Excuse me, sir?" replied Malachi.

"I mean, did they treat you well?"

Then it dawned on Malachi. He was still wearing his Yankee uniform.

"Yes, sir, they treated me just fine," Malachi said in his best northern accent.

"What is your name, son?"

Malachi stood and saluted. He'd rehearsed it so many times, it came out sounding natural. "My name is Sergeant Malachi Jones, from the 304th infantry out of Boston, Mass, sir."

"304th?" the Lieutenant repeated. "It doesn't sound familiar. How did they capture you?"

Malachi was lost for words. Seeing he was in trouble, Captain Malory spoke up. "We found him unconscious, a blow to the head. We nursed him back to health; and he's been our prisoner since."

"And who are you, sir?" Lieutenant Gramm asked.

"Captain Malory, sir."

"Well, Captain Malory, I will show your men the same courtesy you have shown our man, as long as you do what you are told. Is that understood?"

"Yes it is, sir," replied Malory.

"We've collected the guns and put them in the wagon, sir," said Captain Honeycutt.

"Very good," Lieutenant Gramm said. "Captain Honeycutt, this is Sergeant Jones, put him with the rest of your men." He turned to Malachi. "Sergeant Jones, follow Captain Honeycutt's orders. In time, we will find a way to return you to your company."

"Follow me, Jones," Honeycutt said.

"Oh, and Captain, allow the prisoners their backpacks; but I want every pack searched for weapons before they leave this building," Lieutenant Gramm ordered.

"You heard the Lieutenant," Honeycutt shouted. "Search 'em."

Malachi started to look through Captain Malory's backpack. The two men bent low and whispered softly.

"Jones, switch backpacks with me," Captain Malory said.

"What for?" Malachi asked.

"If ya get out of this, you're gonna need your Confederate uniform. Ya don't want to get shot by one of ours."

When they were sure no one was looking, they switched packs. All of Malachi's comrades gave him a quick look of recognition and a wink of the eye for good luck.

"All right," Captain Honeycutt shouted. "Take them outside and line them up two-by-two."

Lined up outside, Lieutenant Gramm addressed them from horseback. "Gentlemen, you are now prisoners of the Union. You will be treated fairly if you cooperate. We march one hundred miles southeast to a prisoner-of-war camp. You will remain there till the end of the war, which, as you know, will be soon. At that time, you will be allowed to return to your homes and families." He looked to Honeycutt. "Captain, begin the march."

Honeycutt raised his arm, brought it down, pointing forward, shouting, "Company...forward....march." With that, the two armies marched side by side heading east.

Lieutenant Gramm and Captain Honeycutt were both on horseback at the head of the caravan, followed by the prisoners and flanked on both sides with armed Yankee soldiers. After that were thirty Yankees marching in double file, and after them was a supply wagon drawn by two mules.

Farther down the road, Malachi, a rifle over his shoulder, worked his way forward and marched next to Captain Malory.

"I'm gotta make a break for it," whispered Malachi. "When we get to wherever they're goin', and they start asking me questions, they're sure to find me out."

"How ya gonna do it?" Malory asked.

"I got a plan. It's a simple one, but I think it'll work. I'll try to get to ya and the boys later on."

"What for?" Malory couldn't see the reason. "Why don't ya work your way back home?"

"This is still my company. Maybe I can help ya escape."

"Don't be a fool, Jones. Save yourself."

"Sorry, Captain, that's my plan."

With that, Malachi worked his way back and returned to the ranks of the Yankee soldiers.

Every so often, Captain Honeycutt steered his horse around the caravan, making sure everything was as it should be. When he came next to Malachi, he slowed down.

"How's it goin', Jones?"

"Just fine, sir."

"Say, Jones, what part of Boston are ya from? I got family up in them parts."

The questions were starting already, questions Malachi had no answers for, so he changed the subject.

"Excuse me, Captain, but I need to see a man about a horse."

"Can't ya hold it, Jones? We'll be stopping to rest in an hour."

"Sorry, Captain. I don't think I can wait another minute, never mind an hour."

"Very well, find yourself a tree over there. When you're done, catch up by running. Don't be long."

"I won't, sir," Malachi said as he broke rank and ran for the trees. Once deep in the woods, Malachi kept running.

When he could run no farther, he slowed down to a brisk walk. By then, the Yankees were sure to know he was missing. Surely, they'd mark him as a deserter and not worth the effort of hunting him down, especially saddled with so many prisoners in tow.

As he moved through the foliage, he looked for something to eat. The mush he ate the night before had long since worn off. He found a few berries and some pine nuts, and he still had a full canteen of water.

When he reached the top of a very high hill, he looked back to view the way he came. Down in the valley below, he saw movement. He strained his eyes to see what it was. When they moved into a clearing, Malachi got a good look at them. He'd been wrong. The Yankees had thought a deserter was worth hunting down. There in the valley were three Yankee soldiers tracking him down. He had to think fast.

He turned to look down the other side of the hill, into the valley before him. There in a clearing was a small troop of Confederate soldiers. He quickly stripped and put on his own uniform and stuffed the Yankee uniform in his backpack. Surely, when his pursuers saw him with other Johnny Rebs and knew they were outnumbered, they'd give up the hunt. He began running down the hill.

When he neared the bottom of the hill and could be seen by those below, they raised their weapons and pointed them at him.

"Halt, who goes there?" shouted one of the men.

"Don't shoot," hollered Malachi, "I'm one of y'all."

As he entered the clearing, approaching them, they continued to keep their aim on him.

"State your name and your business," a sergeant holding a revolver on him demanded.

"Private Malachi Jones with the 5th out of Georgia."

"And how is it we find ya on your lonesome in these parts?" the sergeant asked.

"The Yankees took my company prisoner this morning."

"And ya was just lucky enough to slip away unseen."

"No, it wasn't like that. It's a long and crazy story."

"I'm willin' to listen."

Another of the men spoke up. "Georgia, aye? What's the main crop of Georgia?"

Malachi looked befuddled. "Heck, I don't know. Cotton and peanuts, I guess."

"Is that right?" someone asked the man who posed the question.

"I don't know. I just figured he wouldn't know, if he was a spy."

Another soldier took hold of Malachi's rifle, pulling it from off his shoulder. "Hey, what is this? This is Union issue. What ya doin' with a Yankee rifle?"

One of the soldiers jabs his rifle into Malachi's ribs. "I say we kill him and be done with it. He's either a deserter or a spy. Either way it'd be a better world without him."

"Look!" one of the soldiers shouted, pointing at the top of the hill. At that moment, the three Yankee soldiers who were perusing Malachi came over the ridge.

"See, that must be his partners."

"No, ya got it all wrong," Malachi pleaded. "They've been hunting me down."

The three soldiers pointed down at the clearing. Not thinking it worth taking such a risk, they turned and fled.

"Looks like your friends abandoned ya."

"They're not my friends," Malachi insisted.

"Say, what's this?" one of the soldiers said as he pulled the Yankee uniform out from Malachi's backpack.

"It's not mine. I swear! Ya gotta believe me!"

A fist flew at Malachi, catching him square on the jaw. Then another punch, and then another. Someone hit him in the stomach, and he buckled over. Then with a slam to the back of his head, he fell to the ground. He tried to ward off a barrage of kicks and blows of rifle butts to his face and head, but it was hopeless. Once the pain went away, he slipped into unconsciousness.

****

When he came to, he had no idea how much time had passed. He opened his eyes, but the world was still black. Not a nighttime dimness, but a darkness as if something were covering his eyes. He moved around, and whatever was covering his eyes fell away. He realized it was a dead body that covered him. He looked around and recognized all the Confederate soldiers who had beaten him. They were all dead. Blood and body parts were everywhere, clearly the work of Union heavy artillery.

He tried with all his might to raise himself up, but he was too weak. He landed onto his back. He closed his eyes, trying to summon up strength, when he felt a hand rubbing cool water over his face. He tried to open his eyes, but couldn't. Then he heard a voice.

"Stay still. You're hurt pretty bad. It's a miracle you're still alive. Now, I know this is going to hurt; but I need to move ya. We need to get out of here before the shelling starts again. Are ya ready?"

Malachi just grunted. He felt strong arms embrace him, lifting him up. The voice was right; it did hurt. Again, he lost consciousness.

****

When he regained consciousness, the world was still dark; but this time it was nighttime. A thick blanket covered him, and there was a blazing campfire just inches from his feet.

"How ya feel?" asked the now familiar voice.

Malachi strained to clear his eyesight. He saw the face of an elderly black man sitting on the other side of the campfire. His dark clothing and black skin gave the illusion his face was suspended in midair. His hair was white and closely cropped. A small batch of white covered his chin. His face was long and slender. The flickering flames of the fire made the deep age-cuts in his face dance.

"Who are ya, and what happened?" Malachi asked.

"My name is Marcellus Washington. As to what happened, heavy Yankee artillery is what happened. They have cannons that can reach a mighty distance. It's a miracle ya weren't killed too. The Lord must have something special plannned for ya. And you are...?"

"I'm Private Malachi Jones. My company was captured by the Yankees this morning. I got away, and I been runnin' since."

"Well, Mr. Jones, would ya like somethin' to eat?"

"Thank ya, but I don't think I can chew."

"Yeah, your jaw's gonna be hurtin' for a spell. Ya ain't spittin' up any blood, so I reckon ya be healin' in a few days. Till then, I don't think ya should be movin'."

"Mr. Washington..."

"Call me Marcellus."

"Marcellus, why are ya doin' this?"

"Doin' what?"

"Takin' care of me like this."

"Oh, I don't know. I wasn't taught to turn my back on someone who's hurtin'. Ya know, like the Good Samaritan."

"The good what?" asked Malachi.

"Nothin'. We can talk about it tomorrow." Marcellus stood up. "The fire's gettin' low. Best I be gettin' some more firewood."

The light shone on Marcellus as he stood up. His features became clearer to Malachi. The first thing he noticed was that Marcellus wore a solid white collar.

"Ya a preacher man?" Malachi asked.

"Yeah, how did ya know?" Marcellus brought his hand up to his throat. "Oh yeah, the collar, I forget about it most of the time. I'm so used to it."

"Where's your church?"

"Ain't got one, I just go where the Lord leads me. But we can talk about all this in mornin'. Ya get yourself some rest."

Just the thought of sleep made Malachi's eyes heavy. He could see Marcellus walking off, rummaging for firewood. The next moment, he was fast asleep.

****

Over the next few days, Marcellus slowly nursed Malachi back to health, feeding him and caring for him in everyway. During that time, the two men talked and got to know each other.

"I have a confession to make," Malachi said one night as Marcellus was cooking a squirrel he'd caught earlier in the day.

"Hold on, I'm a preacher not a priest," Marcellus warned playfully.

"It ain't that kind of confession. It's more like admitting somethin' I ain't never admitted before."

"What's that?"

"In all my life, I ain't ever known a black man."

Marcellus laughed. "A good Southern boy like you, and ya ain't never met a black man?"

"I ain't said I never met one. Shoo, my daddy owned slaves on our farm. What I mean is I ain't never sat down and talked friendly with one."

Malachi thought what he said would touch Marcellus' heart, and the old man would smile and make some witty remark. But the opposite was true. Marcellus' face went solemn.

"Your daddy owned slaves?" Marcellus asked coldly.

"Heck yeah, didn't everybody? But our farm was different from most. My daddy was a good man. He was good to his slaves. Our slaves were happy."

"What makes ya think they were happy?" Marcellus asked.

"Well, they never tried to run away. They never complained. They was always smilin'. And most of all, they was always singin'."

Marcellus spoke softly and kindly, but he was firm and to the point. "What would've happened if they ran away, if they even had somewhere to run to?"

Malachi thought for a moment. "I suppose the entire community would have hunted them down."

"How did ya feel when ya were bein' hunted down?" Marcellus asked.

Malachi nodded as he got the point. "I see what ya mean. And I'm sure my daddy wouldn't have put up with complainin'; and if they weren't smilin', Daddy would think they was up to no-good." He shook his head at the folly of his own beliefs as he watched them fall away. Then he asked, "But the singin', why was they singin'?"

Marcellus posed the question, "Why does a man stranded alone on a deserted island sing?"

"I suppose to ward off the fear and the loneliness," Malachi surmised.

"Precisely," Marcellus smiled. "Ya see, I don't believe your daddy was an evil man, but he didn't know what he was gettin' himself into. A great man once said, 'No man can put a chain about the ankle of his fellow man without at last finding the other end fastened to his own neck.' And I don't blame ya, Malachi, for thinking the way ya think, cause of the way ya was raised. Ya need educatin', and I got just the book that's gonna set ya straight," Marcellus said, holding up his Bible.

"But don't the Bible approve of slavery?" Malachi asked.

"Son, ya is gonna be one tough nut to crack, but I believes ya to be worth it." Marcellus opened his Bible, licked his finger, and flipped past the first few pages. "Very well, let us make a start of this. 'In the beginning...'"

****

Each day Malachi grew stronger in body and spirit, thanks to Marcellus. As well, the friendship between the two men grew close and strong. For this reason, it saddens my heart to relate what happened next. There is no excuse, but it's easy to understand. Fear is the strongest demon in the army of Satan, and Malachi still clung to his fear.

Early one morning, Marcellus examined Malachi's wounds. "Ya heal right good. We should be able to move ya in another day or so." Then he placed some food next to Malachi. "I be gone most of the day, so don't fret. I'll be back sometime in the afternoon."

"Where ya goin'?"

"I got somethin' I gotta do, the Lord's work."

"Before ya go, can I ask ya a question?" Malachi asked shyly. Marcellus didn't answer as he stood waiting. "My daddy owned slaves till the day he died. I know that's wrong now. Do ya think my daddy is in heaven?"

Marcellus was quick to answer. "That all depends on your daddy's relationship with the Lord. If you're worried your father didn't get into heaven because he was a sinner, don't bother. All God's children are bad little boys and girls, but we got a good and forgivin' Daddy. If only good people went to heaven then the place would be empty. If your daddy was saved, then he was saved. Once saved, always saved, I always say. That answer your question?"

Malachi shook his head and smiled.

With that, Marcellus walked off into the forest.

Malachi spent the day eating, sleeping, playing his mouth harp, and reading Marcellus' Bible. Late in the day, Marcellus returned with his face and hands filthy.

"What happened?" Malachi asked.

"I figured it was safe enough to return to the valley where I found ya. I went back to take care of the bodies of those Johnny Rebs. I would have liked to bury them, but there was just too many of `em. So I built a fire and burned the bodies."

"Why did ya do that?" Malachi asked. "I mean…I don't understand."

"I know it wasn't a Christian burial, but no man should be left to feed crows. God loves everybody, and I love God. So whatever he loves, I love. It don't matter what their politics were, they deserve respect."

Malachi was dumbfounded.

"Well, if cleanliness is next to godliness, I guess I'm pretty far from the Lord, right now." He pointed north. "There's a pond on the other side of that ridge. I need to get out of these clothes and wash the ash off me. I'll be back in a spell to fix dinner."

Malachi watched Marcellus go over the ridge. Then an idea popped into his head, like lighting lights up a night sky. He knew the scheme was not a very nice one to pull on Marcellus, especially after the way Marcellus had cared for him. A flicker of shame came over him, but he quickly extinguished it.

He was a little woozy when he stood up. He found his backpack, placing the leftover food in it. He inched his way over the ridge and down to the pond. He couldn't see Marcellus because of the high bushes; but he could hear him splashing about in the water, singing as he bathed.

Where are you bound?
Bound for Canaan land

Oh, you must not lie
You must not steal
You must not take the Lord's name in vain
I'm bound for Canaan land

How do you know?

Jesus told me

Marcellus' clothes rested over one of the bushes. Malachi quickly stripped out of his uniform and put on the preacher's clothes. If dressed as a Johnny Reb, he could move safely through Confederate held territory. And if dressed in a Yankee uniform, he could move safely through Union held territory. Perhaps, dressed as a man of the cloth, he could move about freely in every territory.

Your horse is white, your garment is bright

A Slave's Song

You look like a man of war
Raise up your head with courage bold
For your race is almost run

How do you know?
Jesus told me

The thought came to Malachi that leaving Marcellus the way he was, naked, would be cruel. He placed his Rebel uniform where the preacher clothes had been, and then took the Yankee uniform out of his backpack, placing it next to it. He stuffed what little morsels of food there were in both pockets. Again, a twinge of guilt tried to seize him; but he fought against it and won. As much as he cared for the old preacher, he felt a stronger loyalty to his brothers in arms. Perhaps he could be of help to them, maybe even help them escape. He turned to face southeast and began his journey. Now far behind him, he could hear the old man singing.

Although you see me going so
I'm bound for Canaan land
I have trials here below
I'm bound for Canaan land

How do you know? Jesus told me

Three

Down by the Riverside

Malachi's wounds were still hurting, but he pressed on without a moment's rest. He wanted to get as much distance as he could between Marcellus and him. The thought of facing the old preacher after what he'd done for him filled him with shame and embarrassment. But there was no reason to believe Marcellus would follow him.

As he walked through the thick woods, he took pieces of the squirrel meat out of his pockets and ate them. It was best to eat it as soon as possible before it went rancid. He replaced the empty space in his pockets with berries, nuts, and edible roots that he found along the way. Every so often, he'd slip his finger between the clerical collar and his neck to stop it from chafing. He wondered how many years Marcellus was a preacher man to not let a stiff collar bother him or even remembered he wore it.

He came to a small creek. He knelt down and scooped up a handful of water. When he was just about to put it to his lips, he remembered Corporal Hood and his Bible story about Gideon. "Why take chances?" he said out loud, shaking the water from his hand. He stretched flat to the stream and lapped with his tongue like a dog. When he finished he stood up. "Maybe now the Lord will send *me* home."

It seemed strange to be alone. Besides a few stolen moments, he had not been alone for over two years. He felt calm and scared all at once. Strangest of all, he was missing Marcellus' company.

As the day wore on, Malachi felt his not-quite-healed body getting the best of him. Mostly he felt tired, more tired than he'd get from a day's march with the company. As the sun, which he couldn't see for the foliage, began to set, shadows became darker, longer, and more plentiful. He felt as if he were moving around inside the belly of great beast or like Jonah caught in the stomach of a great fish. How dark and lonely must that have been? It must have been frightening. But Malachi thought of something to ward off his fear, his mouth organ. He began to blow a tune, but the notes echoed back sour and distorted. He thought once more about Jonah. Malachi began to understand such fear.

Just before it became too dark to see, he came to the edge of the forest. It opened out to a short green grass plain. Before him was a hill. Not a very large hill, but one he didn't feel like climbing at the moment. It would still be there in the morning. He lay on the ground, pressing his back against a tree. He lifted the collar of Marcellus' black jacket and covered his chest against the coming night chill. He closed his eyes and in no time was fast asleep.

****

Malachi opened his eyes. It was early morning, when the world is still gray. Something woke him up, but he didn't know what. He looked around. He was quite alone. He stood up slowly, his back stiff from spending the night against a tree. Then he realized what woke him, the sound of rolling thunder. He put out his hand, palm up, but didn't feel any rain. Then he heard it again, but it wasn't coming from the sky. It came from the other side of the hill that was before him. How could that be? He imagined some mythical Greek god on the other side of the hill throwing lighting bolts around like a child playing mumbley-peg.

He started slowly up the slope, the sound getting louder. When he neared the summit, he heard the rumbling clearly, and recognized what it was. It wasn't rolling thunder; it was the sound of military drums. At the top of the hill, he looked down below at a large, flat, green field. To his left, were no fewer than one hundred Confederate soldiers. They looked like a ragtag bunch that'd seen too much bloodshed and too little food. Their gray uniforms were tattered and torn, their faces dirty and their hair uncut and unkempt. They had two small cannons.

To his right, was slightly more that one- hundred Yankees. They stood in well-filed ranks like so many toy soldiers, well-feed and ready to scrap. Their clean uniforms like a blue wave in the sea sparkled of gold as the new day's sunlight shone off their buttons. They had one-dozen cannons. Standing behind the cannons were one-dozen drummer boys pounding so hard the very air vibrated, pushing against their chests.

In front of the Confederate troops was a line of six horses on which rode six officers with swords drawn. In front of the Union troops were twenty horses carrying as many officers with their swords drawn, too.

Suddenly, the drumming stopped. A silence fell over the plane that was broken by intervals of a howling wind. Then, like Gabriel announcing the apocalypse, a trumpet blew the attack.

The drums started again. On both sides, the men on horseback galloped forward. Behind them, the foot soldiers ran forward, screaming like banshees. When they were a third of the way on both sides, the cannons started. Malachi flinched with each deafening blast. At first, the cannon fire fell short of their targets. Mounds of ground and turf were flung six feet high. But once the gunners got their bearings, they hit their marks. Weapons flew into the air with hands still gripping them and arms attached to the hands. Blood-soaked blue and gray material soared to the sky, being caught by the high winds. Horses fell, breaking their legs as they landed. Men's bodies began to pile up, covering the green plane.

The Yankees took careful aim and knocked out one of the Confederate cannons. With seven or eight tries, they hit the other cannon. The running infantry began firing their rifles. Men on both sides fell by the row, first one, then the next, and then the next, and so on. Finally, the two infantry lines meet in the middle of the field. The sound of weapons rattled the air and he could hear men grunting.

The cannon fire stopped. Now it was hand-to-hand combat. Bayonets found their mark in the enemy's neck, chest, stomach, and legs. Even from the distance he stood, Malachi could see the blood; he could smell it. Heads began to fall. Though outnumbered, the rebels fought well. It was difficult to tell who was winning. At times the gray uniforms outnumbered the blue. Then the blue outnumbered the gray. Back and forth it went for what seemed like hours till there were few left standing.

Then, as abruptly as it started, the drums stopped; a trumpet blared again, and the fighting stopped. It was impossible to tell who won. The few soldiers left just stood staring at one another, too tired to fight on. Wagons from both sides came out to the field. The few survivors walked about picking up the wounded, tossing them into the wagons. There were just too many dead to stay and bury them, so an hour later, when the wagons where full, both armies walked off the battlefield, turned their back on the many dead, and marched away. Malachi fell to his knees and wept. When he could cry no more, he headed down the hill to the battlefield below.

Malachi walked the perimeter of the battlefield trying to estimate the number of dead. It was impossible. He couldn't enter the circle of bodies for they lay so near one another there was no room for footing. Through the silence, he heard the caw of crows. He looked around to see hundreds of black crows settling on the branches of surrounding trees. They remained perched, staring at their next meal, waiting for Malachi to leave. Finally, a few birds grew tired of waiting, and swooped down on the bodies. Malachi ran at them, shouting and waving his arm. They flew back to their perches.

Then he remembered something Marcellus had said. "No man should be left to feed crows. God loves everybody, and I love God. So whatever he loves, I love. It don't matter what their politics were, they deserve respect." Inwardly, he agreed.

He began walking the perimeter, moving the bodies to the center of the field. Around and around he went, moving the bodies a few feet at a time, till he'd piled them high up. He went off into the woods and collected dead wood, twenty armfuls. He rummaged through the top pockets of some of the dead soldiers. Surely, one or more of them were smokers. It took only three pockets to find a pipe, tobacco, and some matches. He lit one of the soldier's pant leg and then another's shirt cuff. The flames quickly consumed the uniforms from one man to the next, then the wood caught fire, and in no time the entire field was a funeral pyre. The smoke rose to the sky; sparks and ashes danced in the air. As he watched the fire, Malachi said a silent prayer. He asked for their souls to be accepted and for the Lord to forgive the entire world for what it had become. There was nothing else to do, so he walked off the field and into the woods.

He hadn't gone far, only a few yards into the woods, when something caught his eyes. Seated there on the ground, leaning against the trunk of a large tree was a dead Yankee soldier. It seemed he was badly wounded in battle, stumbled off into the woods, collapsing at the foot of the tree where he died, perhaps no more than a few minutes earlier. He reached out, placing his hand on the soldier's forehead. There was still warmth to be felt. Malachi stood staring at the man's face, examining every feature. His blue eyes stared without blinking, a cold, dead stare. He wore a thick, bushy mustache that grew along the sides of his mouth to his chin.

Malachi got down and knelt next to the body. He reached into the dead man's top pocket. He took out two items: the man's wallet and an envelope.

There wasn't much in the wallet. The man was William Martin, from Tarrytown, New York. He belonged to the local chess club and was a Presbyterian. Within the wallet was a small photograph of a woman with dark hair and features, holding a baby in her arms. It dawned on Malachi that this was a man with hopes, dreams, and plans for the future. He had loves and likes, good and bad thoughts and deeds. In short, he was no different from any other man, no different from Malachi.

"Your family?" Malachi asked, holding the photograph to the dead man. The man's wide-open eyes made Malachi feel uneasy. Malachi reached over and shut his eyes. Then he opened the envelope, took out a letter, and began to read.

Dear Willie,

Words cannot convey the emptiness your absence has left in this family. The days are colder, and nights are dark and long. Many times in the night I wake and reach across the bed half hoping my hand will find you, but I grasp only air, and in my disappointment I cry myself awake.
Little Thomas is not as little as you remember him to be. He has been walking clumsily for many months now and, to my dismay, can grasp articles within arms reach. His round baby face is no more as the child in him emerges. He looks more like you each day. I speak to him constantly, not just to teach him speech, but it keeps the loneliness at bay.

My sweet darling, I miss you beyond understanding. I close my eyes, and I see only your face. The fear of losing you has consumed me. Forgive me, but I now play the most foolish of games, to keep my sanity. I pretend that you are dead, and that I will never see you again. I know this is foolish, but it keeps away the madness.

I figure, when they come to tell me you have died, I can reply, 'Yes, I know.' But also, when you come home to us I can claim it to be a miracle. My husband has risen like Lazarus.

And you will come home, my darling, I know you will. I've heard talk the war will end soon. I pray it be so. Oh, please come home, my love. Your son is growing so much that his little bed is too small, and your wife's bed is too large.

Your,
Linda

Malachi returned the wallet, the photograph, and the letter to William's pocket.

"I'm so sorry ya lost your life, my brother," Malachi said as he stood up. "It seems it was a very good life." Malachi reached down, pulling at William's jacket. "Come, ya need to join the others." He placed the dead man over his shoulder and carried him out of the woods, onto the battlefield, and laid him onto the fire.

Malachi turned and headed back into the woods.

****

The forest became dense once more. The closeness of the trees blocked out most of the sunlight. Now and then a flake of ash would fall from the sky like gray snow. He knew it was from the funeral pyre, now miles behind. In his mind, he could still see the face of the dead, especially that of poor Willie who sadly died alone. He could feel the dead staring at the back of his head; but unlike Lot's wife, he never looked back.

As the day waned on, he continued his journey. When darkness settled around him, he continued; though he felt tired and hungry, he marched on. He wanted to put as much distance between him and that battlefield as possible.

It was a moonless night, which made going difficult. Suddenly, he heard singing, a single voice singing. It sounded like a young woman's voice.

Oh, hallelujah to the lamb
Down by the river
The Lord is on the givin' hand
Down by the riverside

Oh, we'll wait 'til Jesus comes
Down by the river
Oh, we'll wait 'til Jesus comes
Down by the riverside

Stepping out of the woods, Malachi found himself on the edge of a calm river. It wasn't very wide, but it would be a hard swim to the other side. A few yards upstream, on the banks of the river, he saw a large raft made of logs. It was too dark to make out their features, but he could see an old black man on the raft seated on a bucket. Next to him stood a young black man, tall and lean, maybe fifteen-years-old. The lad leaned on a long pole that was in the water. It wasn't a woman; it was the young man who was singing.

Oh, we are pilgrims here below
Down by the river
Oh, soon to glory we will go
Down by the riverside

Oh, we'll wait 'til Jesus comes
Down by the river
Oh, we'll wait 'til Jesus comes

Down by the riverside

He stopped singing when Malachi came into view. He stood up straight, putting a firm grip on the pole. He spoke not a word, waiting for Malachi to make the first move.

"Evenin'," said Malachi.

"Evenin', sir," said the lad.

"How much is it for a ride across river?" asked Malachi.

"It's free for any man of the cloth, sir."

"That's mighty kind of ya."

"Ain't got no church in these parts," said the young man. "No place to give our tithe, so the least we can do is give a preacher man a ride cross river, now and then."

He reached out, offering Malachi his hand, helping him onboard. Then he took the poll, pushed it hard against the riverbank, and they were underway.

The young man remained silent as he pushed the pole down to the mud below, guiding them to the other side. A third of the way across, Malachi tried his hand at conversation.

"What's your name, son?" he asked.

"Hershel, sir."

"This your raft, Hershel?"

"No, sir, it belongs to my daddy."

"Is this your daddy?" Malachi asked, pointing to the old man seated on the bucket.

"No, he's a friend of my daddy."

Malachi looked at the old man. He wore no shoes, and a floppy hat that covered his face, which he held cast down. Strange enough, he wore a Confederate uniform's pair of pants.

"And what is your name, sir?" asked Malachi.

"The name's Marcellus."

The old man looked up smiling at Malachi. It was Marcellus! The shock was so great, Malachi jumped back and fell off the raft and into the water.

Hershel brought the pole around, thrusting it at Malachi. "Here, take hold," shouted Hershel.

Hand over hand, Malachi pulled himself in. When he was at the edge of the raft, Marcellus pulled him in like an overgrown carp.

"Ya scared the bajebars out of me," Malachi said to Marcellus.

"Good," said Marcellus. "Now ya know how I felt when I came out of the water only to find a Rebel and a Yankee uniform to wear. I'm not sure if it's safe for a black man to wear either one in these parts."

When they reached the shore, Malachi jumped from the raft and headed up the slope to flat ground, followed by Marcellus and Hershel.

"Gather up more firewood, son. I'll get a fire started," Marcellus told Hershel.

Malachi found their campsite. In no time, Marcellus had a roaring fire going.

"Well, take off those wet clothes, before ya catch your death," Marcellus told Malachi who sent him a questioning look. "Don't worry," said Marcellus. When they're dry, ya can put them back on. They're yours now."

Malachi stripped down. Marcellus tossed him a blanket. Malachi wrapped it around his body. Marcellus placed the wet clothes on the opposite side of the campfire to dry. Malachi sat down on the ground shivering, getting as close to the fire as he could. Hershel returned with an armful of dry wood and placed it on the ground.

"I suppose you're hungry?" Marcellus asked, offering Malachi a piece of meat.

"I suppose that's squirrel," said Malachi.

"Nah, it's fish, easier to catch."

Malachi took a piece and savored it, chewing slowly.

"Why ya still treatin' me good?" Malachi asked.

"Why shouldn't I?" Marcellus asked.

"Because I robbed your clothes, that's why."

Marcellus laughed. "Shoo, if I took it out on everyone who done me wrong in my life, I'd need another life just to get her done. Besides, ya ain't special. Ya ain't the only sinner in the world. Anyways, the Lord's got funny ways. He can take somethin' bad and use it for somethin' good. And I think that's just what he's up to in this here situation."

"How's that?" Malachi asked.

"Too late to talk now," said Marcellus. He turned to see that Herschel was already fast asleep. "Best get some shut-eye; we'll talk about it in the mornin'."

Malachi didn't have to be told twice, he was so tired. He stretched out and closed his eyes. The last thing he heard was Marcellus singing soft and low.

He got the whole world in his hands
He got the big, round world in his hands
He got the whole world in his hands

He got the wind and the rain
He got the little baby
He got you and me, sister
He got you and me, brother
He got the whole world in his hands

****

Malachi could have slept away the morning. But the sweet smell of bacon cooking made his stomach rumble so loud, it woke him up. He opened his eyes. Hershel was nowhere to be found. Marcellus was kneeling at the fire, using a fork to turn piece of bacon in an iron skillet.

"How do ya like your bacon?" Marcellus asked.

"It don't matter none."

"Grab those cups and pour us some coffee."

As Malachi poured the coffee, Marcellus broke out in song.

"Ain't it a little early in the day to start singing?" Malachi pleaded.

"It ain't never too early or too late for singin', especially when ya singin' to the Lord," replied Marcellus. "Beside, the Good Book says to pray without ceasing. What better way to do that than to do it in song. Ya sing all day, 'hallelujah'." He burst into song again.

I sing because I'm happy
I sing because I'm free
For his eye is on the sparrow
And I know he watches me

Whenever I am tempted
Whenever clouds arise
When song gives place to sighin'
When hope within me dies
I draw closer to Him
For care he sets me free
His eye is on the sparrow
And I know he watches me
Yes, his eye is on the sparrow
And I know he watches me

****

Hershel returned with a string of fish he'd just caught. He placed them down, poured himself some coffee, and sat down.

"Good work, son, good work. That's gonna make a fine lunch, Hershel," Marcellus said. He turned and placed his hand on Malachi's clothing. "They're dry as a bone. Ya might as well put them back on," he told Malachi.

"Haven't we better have that talk first?" Malachi asked.

"We do need to talk," said Marcellus, "but first put your clothes on. We can talk while we eat."

Malachi took hold of his clothes, holding them in his arms. Still wrapped in the blanket, he sat down; and Marcellus served bacon, bread, and coffee for the three of them.

"So let's hear your side of it," Marcellus said.

"I just want to get to my company. I gotta find 'em."

"From what you've told me, I imagine they're takin' them down to Shannon city. The Yankees have an outpost there with a holdin' area for keepin' rebel prisoners. I go there every so often to preach to the folks down there. Lotta plantation slaves that ain't gotta a place to call home since the farms got ruined by the war. It's 'bout a week's walk southeast from here. But that don't excuse ya none, ya in big trouble now, son."

31

"I'm sorry. I'll give ya back your clothes," Malachi begged.

"I told ya to keep 'em. They're yours now. When I say you're in trouble, I don't mean with me. I'm talkin' 'bout the Lord. Right now, ya on his bad side; and I wouldn't want to be ya, if I was ya. Goin' 'round dressed as a preacher man and not preachin', ya just askin' for the wrath of the Lord to come on ya."

"What can I do?" Malachi asked, taking it all very seriously.

"Well, I'd say ya owe the Lord. Ya wearing his uniform, but ya ain't servin'. If ya gonna dress like a preacher man, ya gonna have to start preachin'."

"I can't do that," Malachi said. "Jus' because ya dress like a preacher don't make ya a preacher. They say clothes make the man. Well, not in this case."

"That's because ya ain't got all the equipment," Marcellus said, handing him a Bible. "This here's what ya need."

"That ain't gonna do me no good," said Malachi. "I done read through the Bible a month of Sundays and I still can't make head or tails of it."

"That's because ya ain't ever had the right teacher," replied Marcellus.

"And I suppose that would be you?"

Marcellus laughed. "Not me. I'm talkin' 'bout the greatest teacher there is. I'm talkin' 'bout the Spirit of the Lord. Ya Christian, ain't ya?"

"I'd say I was," Malachi answered back.

"And have ya every been baptized?"

"No, I ain't, but so what?"

"See, that's your problem. Ya ain't ever been baptized, so ya ain't ever received the Spirit. Once ya got the Spirit, ya can understand the Bible; and ya have the power to preach it."

"So how do I get baptized?" Malachi asked.

Marcellus pointed. "We got a river full of water. Ya got two willin' brothers here with ya. The Lord's in his heaven, and all's right with the world. We can get this done right here and now. Come on."

Marcellus stood up and walked down to the river; Malachi and Hershel followed. When they got to the bank, Marcellus walked into the river up to his waist.

"Hershel," he cried, "come in here and help me with the dunkin'."

"Yes, sir," said Hershel as he removed his shirt.

It was then Malachi got a good look at Hershel's back.

"My Lord, son, what happened to your back? It's all scared," Malachi exclaimed.

"The lash, sir," Hershel said. "Massa gave me the whip for breakin' a plate in the kitchen. I dropped it when I was washin' it."

"What kind of man whips a child for breakin' a plate?" Malachi asked to the sky.

"Don't know, sir," replied Hershel. "He's long dead. The Yankees got 'em."

"I'm so sorry, Hershel," Malachi whispered.

"Don't be, sir; ya didn't do it. Besides, it don't hurt none no more, 'cept when it rains."

"Come stand by me, Hershel," Marcellus called him in.

Hershel waded in, standing next to Marcellus. Malachi dropped the blanket and stood there in his long johns. Then he ran into the water splashing all the way. Marcellus and Hershel placed their hands on his shoulders.

"Hold on, brother. Ya gonna be a new creature in the Lord." Then Marcellus began to sing.

I tol' Jesus it would be all right
If He changed my name

Jesus tol' me I would have to live humble
If He changed my name

Jesus tol' me that the world would be 'gainst me
If He changed my name

But I tol' Jesus it would be all right
If He changed my name

"Do ya believe in the Three-Part God, and that Jesus is one of `em?" Marcellus asked.

"I do," replied Malachi.

"Do ya renounce Satan and all his works and look to Jesus as your savior?"

"I do."

"Do ya promise to preach the good news wherever and whenever?"

"I do."

"Then I baptize ya in the name of the Father, the Son, and the Holy Spirit."

With that, they pulled Malachi under the water. They held him down for a longer period of time than Malachi felt comfortable with; but then they let him go; he came up with a deep breath, taking in the sweet morning air.

"Congratulations," Marcellus said, "how do ya feel, any different?"

Malachi thought for a moment. "About the same as I did before, only wetter."

"Don't worry. For some folks it takes a little time. Some people come up talkin' in tongues; they're so full of the Spirit. For others, it comes on them slowly. Now that ya has the Spirit, ya can read the Bible and understand it because the Spirit will teach ya. And ya can preach the good news, because it won't only be you talkin', it'll be the Spirit of the Lord. If ya let him, he'll guide ya through everything…good guidance, too."

Back on shore, they all sat close to the fire to dry off. When the sun was high in the sky, Malachi got dressed.

"Well, I guess I best be goin'," he announce to his two companions, holding his new Bible.

They stood to say their goodbyes. Hershel shook Malachi's hand.

"It was a pleasure to meet ya, sir," Hershel said.

"The pleasure was all mine, Hershel."

Marcellus stood smiling before Malachi.

"Ya take care of yourself out there, ya hear? Don't forget to study your Bible, everyday. Ya got the Spirit now so ya shouldn't have any problems no more to handle alone. Don't forget to preach the Good News along the way and when ya get to wherever it is the Lord is sendin' ya to."

It took a long while before Malachi could talk; there was a lump in his throat.

"I don't know how to thank ya for savin' my life. As long as I wear these clothes, I'll make ya proud."

"Just make the Lord proud," said Marcellus.

"That's not all," said Malachi. "I'm just gonna come right out and say it. I ain't ever been close to a black person before in my life. It makes me think that maybe we ain't that much different. I'm gonna miss ya, Marcellus. I really mean that. I feel like you're my friend, like you're my...my..."

Marcellus finished the sentence. "Brother. Don't be afraid to say it. That's what we are...brothers."

The two men hugged.

"So long, my brother," said Malachi.

"May the Lord bless and keep you, Brother Malachi."

In that moment, something changed in Malachi. Perhaps it was the Spirit. He wasn't sure. Suddenly, skin color didn't mean a hill of beans. Malachi turned, faced southeast, and marched out of the clearing and into the woods. He could hear Marcellus singing.

> *Climb up d' mountain, children*
> *Ya didn't come here to stay*
> *And if I never see ya again*
> *Gonna meet ya on de judgment day*

> *Hebrew in the fiery furnace*
> *And they began to pray*
> *And de good Lord smote de fire out*
> *Oh, wasn't dat a mighty day*
> *Good Lord, wasn't dat a mighty day*

> *Daniel went in de lion's den*
> *And he began to pray*
> *And de angels of de Lord locked de lion's jaw*
> *Oh, wasn't dat a mighty day*
> *Good Lord, wasn't dat a mighty day*

> *Climb up d' mountain, children*
> *Ya didn't come here to stay*

A Slave's Song

And if I never see ya again
Gonna meet ya on de judgment day

Four

Is Master Goin' to Sell Us Tomorrow?

Call me crazy, because I just might be. But to tell the truth, in time, Malachi did feel different, and he blamed it all on the Spirit. He felt important because, for the first time in his life, he felt he had purpose and direction. As for the Bible, which he'd tried to read dozens of times and always struck him as irrelevant pages of so much mishmash that made no sense, now the words jumped off the pages at him. Their meaning clear and precise; they stuck in his brain like his own name. He became hungry for the word. He'd promise himself he'd stop three times a day to read awhile. Only, by the end of the day he realized he'd stopped to read at least ten times. He even read at night sitting close to the campfire. He remembered Marcellus saying he'd become a new creature, and he believed it.

Oh, don't get me wrong. Malachi wasn't a top drawer preacher, not by a long shot. But he was showing promise. The Good Book tells us that to those given much, much is expected. Well, it seemed the Lord was fixing to use Malachi sooner than he anticipated, for a longer time than he could imagine, and in ways he never envisioned.

It was late in the afternoon. Malachi found himself walking along a country road. To one side were the remains of what used to be a long wooden fence. Beyond that lay the ghost of what was once a large cotton field, now dried and withered from neglect.

He walked on. Up ahead was a rundown old shack, dilapidated and tilting slightly to the right. As he approached, he heard a man singing, accompanied by what sounded like an out-of-tune guitar.

Dem bones, dem bones, dem dry bones
Dem bones, dem bones, dem dry bones
Don't ya hear the word of the Lord?

Toe bone connected to the foot bone
Foot bone connected to the leg bone
Leg bone connected to the knee bone
Don't ya hear the word of the Lord?

Leg bone connected to the knee bone
Knee bone connected to the thigh bone
Thigh bone connected to the hip bone
Don't ya hear the word of the Lord?

Hip bone connected to the backbone
Backbone connected to the shoulder bone

A Slave's Song

Shoulder bone connected to the neck bone
Don't ya hear the word of the Lord?

When Malachi came into view of the old man sitting on the porch, he stopped singing and held his guitar. He was a lanky old fellow; more bone than flesh, which made his song all the more poignant. He stared at Malachi waited for him to make the first move.

"Howdy, mind if I set a spell?" Malachi asked with a smile.

The old man remained silent.

"I really enjoyed your singin', old-timer."

Still no word did he speak.

"What's goin' on out here? What's all the..." a middle-aged black woman said as she stepped out of the shack and onto the porch, holding a dishrag. "Why, Daddy, why didn't ya tell me we had company, and a preacher man, too."

"He ain't no preacher man," growled the old man. "I ain't ever seen no white preacher."

"That's because all ya ever been in was a black church. They got white preachers too, Daddy; just ya never seen one." She smiled at Malachi. "Ya have to forgive my father, he's kind of set in his ways."

"Ain't nothin' to ask forgiveness for, my daddy, Lord rest his soul, was set in his ways, too. He probably would have agreed with your daddy. My name's Malachi Jones. I'm just passin' through. Would ya be so kind as to give me a drink of water?"

"Shoo, we'd be please to, but come inside; we'd be twice as pleased to have ya stay for supper."

"Gee, ma'am, that's might kindly of ya, but I couldn't impose."

"Ya not be denying us the Lords blessin' for taken care of one of his own, now would ya, Reverend?"

The smell of country cooking hit Malachi's nose. His stomach began to growl.

"Well, ma'am, since ya put it that way, I can't say no."

Malachi stepped up to the porch, past the old man and his stares, and entered the house. There was an old woman and a young girl preparing food in the kitchen area.

"My name is Naomi," said the woman. "And this is my mother, Mrs. Jackson. Ya already met my father. And this here is my precious daughter, Kathleen. Momma, this is Reverend Jones."

Naomi was a fine-looking woman. Her smile was straight, bright, and constant. House and farm chores had given her large muscular arms, and her calves were wide. She wore a housedress that was old but clean and well-kept.

Little Kathleen was a shy child who would look at you; and when you looked back, she'd look away. This was disappointing because her eyes were clear, deep, and lovely with eyelashes a mile long.

Old Mrs. Jackson was a tiny, frail woman. A long life had left her used up. The skin on her thin arms waved as she moved them. Her back was hunched; she moved slowly and painfully. Despite this, she carried herself with an air of a strong character and a wise soul.

"It's a pleasure to meet ya, Reverend," the old woman said, smiling. The young girl curtseyed politely.

Malachi wasn't expecting to be called Reverend Jones. It threw him off for a moment. "It's a pleasure to meet you both," said Malachi.

"We'll eat as soon as my husband, Jeremiah, and my son, Noah, return from hunting. They should be home any moment."

"Oh, maybe we should wait for your husband's permission for me to stay for supper?"

"Nonsense," Naomi laughed. "I know my husband like I know me. We'd be pleased to have a preacher for supper. Now, why don't ya just go sit over there in the good chair, and rest a spell."

"I see ya got your Good Book at your side, Reverend," said Mrs. Jackson. "Would ya please honor us with a readin'?"

"It would be my pleasure, ma'am," Malachi said as he sat down in what he surmised to be the good chair, opened his Bible to Psalms, and began to read aloud.

A half hour later, Jeremiah and his son came walking through the door, each holding a pheasant. Jeremiah looked surprised when he saw Malachi, but he smiled.

"This here's Reverend Jones, dear. I've invited him to supper with us. Reverend Jones, this is my husband, Jeremiah, and our son, Noah."

"It's a pleasure to meet you, sir," Jeremiah said as the two men shook hands. "If ya give me a minute to wash up, we can sit down to supper."

As Malachi watched the father and son go off to wash, he realized he had been mistaken. When Naomi introduced the two older people as her mother and father, she meant her in-laws. Jeremiah was the very image of his father, dark skinned, tall, and lanky, but with his mother's eyes and smile. Hard labor had chiseled his arms and chest to that of an Adonis. Noah was a stocky lad, no more than an inch shorter than his father. You could tell he was a growing boy. His clothes fit him tight, and his sleeves and pant legs were too short. He was as handsome as his younger sister, Kathleen, was pretty.

They sat at a long table with Jeremiah seated at the head and Naomi at the other end closest to the kitchen. On one side of the table sat Mr. and Mrs. Jackson; on the other, Noah sat closest to his father and Kathleen near her mother with Malachi between them.

"Reverend, it's seldom we're blessed with a guest, let alone a preacher, which makes us twice blessed. If you'd be so kind as to lead us in sayin' grace," Jeremiah asked.

In that instant, Malachi deeply missed Marcellus, and wished he were there. The Good Book tells us iron sharpens iron; and at that moment, Malachi was feeling mighty dull. He wondered how Marcellus would say grace. Then he remembered Marcellus told him that if he let the Spirit, the Spirit would do most of the talking. Besides, how hard could it be? Keep it simple.

Malachi began to pray. "Dear Lord, we praise ya and thank ya for this bounty. Please, bless it that it may nourish our bodies to do your will. And I ask that ya bless this family who has opened their home and table to one of your servants. Amen."

"Amen," they answered as one. Then before another word was spoken, the family gathered hands. The children took hold of Malachi's hands. They all smiled, lifted their eyes, and began to sing.

The Lord is my Shepherd
He leads me day by day
He feeds me when I'm hungry
And hears me when I pray

John on the isle of Patmos
Looked over in the Glory land
He heard the Angels singin'
And shouted Hallelujah! Amen!

Sometimes my way gets cloudy
My path is all confused
I set my face toward heaven
Determined to go through

The Lord is my Shepherd
He leads me day by day
He feeds me when I'm hungry
And hears me when I pray

Amen! Amen! Amen!

When they finished singing, they began passing the food around.

"That's just a family tradition…signin', that is. We're a musical family," Jeremiah said with pride.

"I know," said Malachi. "I heard your father earlier."

"Maybe we can get him to sing after dinner," Jeremiah replied. "Sweetheart, it all looks good," he said to his wife and then looked to Malachi. "So tell us, Reverend, what brings ya to these parts?"

"I have business to attend to in Shannon city."

"Shannon city, that's quite a hike. Might I ask, Reverend, if ya have a place to stay for the night?"

"The weather's been good. I don't mind sleepin' under the stars."

"Not tonight. You're welcome to spend the night here. Noah wouldn't mind givin' up his bed for one night, would ya, Noah?"

"Wait on, now," Malachi said as soon as he finished swallowing. "I thank ya kindly for the offer, but…"

"I won't hear it any other way," Jeremiah interrupted.

"I tell ya what," Malachi said. "I'll take ya up on your offer on two conditions. I will not put anyone out of their beds. That cozy chair ya got is just fine for me, and that your daddy sings us some songs after supper."

"I wish you'd reconsider about the bed," Jeremiah claimed. "But if that's how ya want it, so be it. As for my father singin' after supper, ya never have to ask him twice."

The food was plentiful, but simple. There was just enough meat to make it filling with bread and vegetables they grew themselves. After supper, the women cleaned up, and the men-folk went out on the porch. In time, the women joined them.

It was a comfortable evening. Jeremiah was right, it didn't take much to coax his father to play his guitar and sing. Malachi was not prepared for the songs he was about to hear. These were not songs that folks performed in the circles Malachi socialized in. Father Jackson's voice was low and harsh.

> *Slavery chain done broke at last*
> *Broke at last, broke at last*
> *Slavery chain done broke at last*
> *Going to praise God till I die*

As he continued singing, he looked to Malachi to see how he'd react to lyrics only black slaves knew, heard, and sang.

> *Way down in-a dat valley*
> *Prayin' on my knees*
> *Told God about my troubles*
> *And to help me ef-a He please*

> *I did tell him how I suffer*
> *In de dungeon and de chain*
> *And de days were with head bowed down*
> *And my broken flesh and pain*

Again, Malachi felt Father Jackson's stare. He answered the old man's question with music. He took out his mouth harp, and began to play along.

> *I did know my Jesus heard me*
> *`Cause de Spirit spoke to me*
> *And said, "Raise my child, your chillun*
> *And you shall be free*

> *'I done `ppoint one mighty captain*
> *For a marshall all my hosts*
> *And to bring my bleedin' ones to me*
> *And not one shall be lost"*

A Slave's Song

Slavery chain done broke at last
Broke at last, broke at last
Slavery chain done broke at last
Goin' to praise God till I die

As the last note faded, the small group applauded and everyone turned to compliment Malachi on his playing. The old man's smile was as wide as a river. He had made a new friend.

"Ya play a mighty fine harp there, Reverend," said the old man.

"I ain't ever heard that song before," Malachi said.

The old man laughed. "It don't surprise me none. I wouldn't suspect they'd be singin' that song in a white man's church. No offence, Reverend."

"None taken," Malachi answered. "Say, do ya know any other songs like that?'

The old man smiled, nodded, bringing the guitar close to him.

Mother, is master goin' to sell us tomorrow?
Yes, yes, yes!
O, watch and pray

Going to see us in Georgia?
Yes, yes, yes!
O, watch and pray

Farewell, mother, I must be leavin' you
Yes, yes, yes!
O, watch and pray

Mother, don't grieve after me
No, no, no!
O, watch and pray

Mother, I'll meet you in heaven
Yes, my child!
O, watch and pray

A silence fell over the small group. The song of cicada filled the air. Reluctantly, Malachi spoke.

"Was that how it was?" he asked.

All but the children placed their hands over their mouths to hide their snickers.

"Reverend Jones," said the old man, "it was worse than that, so much worse. We was lucky. Our family was able to stay together. Some slaves got sold as much as two or three times in their lives. Husbands and wives separated forever. Children torn from their mother's arms, entire family sold to the four corners, never to see one another again. I tell ya, Reverend, there are some things in this world worse than death, things that make death a blessing."

Jeremiah stood up and stretched. "Well, I don't know 'bout you folks, but it's been a long day for me."

"Children, get ready for bed," Naomi said. "Reverend Jones, you're welcome to go to sleep whenever ya feel like it."

"Thank ya, ma'am, I think I'll hit the hay, now. I need to get an early start in the morning." He stood, turning to the elders. "It's been a pleasure. Thank ya, and goodnight."

Inside, he found a blanket and a pillow in the good chair. He settled in.

Jeremiah tapped him on the shoulder. "I've gotta get up before dawn. If ya like, I can wake ya then."

"I'd like that. Thank ya, Jeremiah."

Just before he dozed off, Malachi heard the old couple enter the house and tiptoe past him.

"Goodnight, Reverend," they whispered.

"Goodnight," Malachi replied. "Ah, Mr. Jackson…?"

"Yes, Reverend?"

Malachi hesitated before speaking. "I'm sorry…I didn't know."

"Don't feel sorry. Ya wasn't the cause of it. Ya didn't even know it was happenin'; and even if ya did, ya couldn't have stopped it. Goodnight, Reverend."

****

The room was silent and the world was still dark when Jeremiah gently shook Malachi awake.

"Ya sure ya don't want to wait a few more hours and have breakfast with my family?" whispered Jeremiah.

"Thank ya, but I need to get goin'."

The two men slowly made their way out of the house and away from the porch. The sun was still below the horizon. Jeremiah was holding a fishing rod and a small sack.

"I figured I try my hand at the old creek and do some fishin'. They bite better in the early morning." He handed Malachi the sack. "Here, the wife wanted ya to have this. It's just some biscuits and dried meat; it'll be good on the road."

"Thank ya," Malachi said in a low voice. "You folks have been so kind. Thank ya, again."

"If ya ever in these parts again, you're welcome anytime. Well, be seein' ya. Goodbye, Reverend."

"Goodbye to ya, Brother Jeremiah."

With that, the two men turned, faced opposite directions, and began walking.

A Slave's Song

****

Less than an hour later, as Malachi made his way down the road, he heard the sound of footsteps behind him. Whoever was behind him was running; the footsteps were loud, fast, coming up on him quickly. Not wanting to take any chances, Malachi got off the road and hunkered down behind some bushes. The footsteps were coming closer. He could hear the runner breathing heavily, panting and puffing.

As the runner approached, he realized it was a young black man. Malachi got a good look at him as he rushed by. It was Noah. Malachi came out of hiding, and shouted up the road.

"Noah, here I am. What's wrong?"

The lad turned around, ran to him, stopping a few feet in front of him. He was all sweaty. He bent over with his hands on his thighs, trying to catch his breath.

"Momma said to fetch ya....need...need a preacher for a funeral."

"Funeral? Who died? Was it your grandfather?"

"No, it was grandma. She didn't wake up this mornin'. Momma said if ya don't mind comin' back, we could use a preacher."

"Does your father know?"

"Momma made me fetch him first."

Malachi wasn't sure what he should do, only that he couldn't let down this sweet family. He silently prayed that Marcellus was right about the Spirit doing the talking because he had no idea what he'd say when he got there.

"Well, let's head back," Malachi said. "I can walk fast, but I certainly can't run all the way. Let's go."

They headed back the way they came. An hour later, they could see the old shack. As they approached, Malachi saw Jeremiah standing in the middle of the road, waiting. Malachi stopped before him. Jeremiah's eyes were red from crying.

"I'm so sorry to hear about your mother, Jeremiah."

Jeremiah reached out for Malachi, threw his arms around him, pulling him in close. "Thank ya for doin' this. It would have made momma happy."

At the house, the old man sat on the porch, holding his guitar, not singing but silently staring at the sky. He half-smiled at Malachi as he walked by. Inside, Jeremiah pointed to a door.

"My wife and daughter are in there preparin' momma for her journey home. Noah and I are off to dig the grave. We'll be back soon." With that he left.

Malachi walked softly up to the door and gently knocked. "Mrs. Jackson, it's me, Reverend Jones."

The door opened slowly. Inside, the curtains were drawn; the room was dark save for a single lit candle. Naomi and Kathleen dipped towels in a basin of water. They carefully washed the old woman and fixed her hair.

"Poor dear didn't wake up this mornin'," Naomi said. "She never had more than two dresses in her life. This here's her finer. We do appreciate ya doin' this for us, Reverend. Momma was strong in her belief. She always wanted a send-off with a preacher on hand. But she never thought it would happen. I guess your bein' in these parts is a Godsend."

When they finished, they sat down on the edge of the bed and waited.

Another hour passed and Jeremiah entered the room.

"It's dug. Is she ready?"

Naomi began to weep. "We don't even have so much as a box to put the dear soul in."

"It's all right," Jeremiah said. "Ya got her lookin' so pretty. Why would we want to hide her away in a box? Lord knows she carried me for years. The least I can do is to carry her to her final restin' place."

He came along side of the bed and scooped her up in his arms. Naomi and Kathleen followed with Malachi behind them.

On the porch, Jeremiah stood holding his mother. He looked at his father. "It's time, Daddy."

The old man looked up through sorrowful eyes. "Can I bring my guitar? I'd like to sing a song."

"Momma always liked your singin'. Ain't no reason to believe that's changed."

The small group walked slowly behind the house and up a hill where a lone willow tree stood. At the foot of the tree was the grave.

"Let me help ya," said Malachi as he took the old woman from Jeremiah. He held her in his arms as Jeremiah shimmied down into the grave. With the help of Noah, Malachi handed Jeremiah his mother. He carefully placed her on the ground and climbed back out of the grave. They all stood with bowed heads and folded hands. They waited on Malachi.

He stood at the head of the grave, his hands folded. But, his head wasn't bowed. He was looking to the sky. Inwardly, he prayed a silent prayer. "Oh, dear Lord, these are such good people. They love ya so much. They never ask for much, just a few kind words. Please send down your Spirit to guide me."

Malachi bowed his head and spoke. "Lord, we ask your forgiveness, as we cry tears of sorrow and of loss, for this woman is well loved. We will miss her. But you loved her first, and you loved her best. So we commend her spirit to you. Take her in your loving arms and carry her to her just reward. Give her rest. Tell her to be patient, for life is short; and we will all be united again in the sweet by and by. Amen."

The others echoed, "Amen."

The old man stood at the foot of the grave, bringing his guitar to his chest. But it was too much for him to go on. His hands shook, his throat tightened, as tears filled his eyes and poured down his cheeks. Seeing his father so helpless, Jeremiah walked to his father's side, placing his hand on his shoulder. Then Jeremiah began to sing.

I think I heard him say, when he was struggling up the hill
I think I heard him say, take my mother home

A Slave's Song

Then I'll die easy, take my mother home
I'll die so easy, take my mother home

I think I heard him say, when they was raffling off His clothes
I think I heard him say, take my mother home
I think I heard him cry, when they was nailing in the nails
I think I heard him cry, take my mother home

I'll die this death on Calvary, ain't gonna die no more
I'll die on Calvary, ain't gonna die no more
Ain't gonna die no more

I think I heard Him say, when He was giving up the ghost
I think I heard Him say, please, take my mother home
Please, take my mother home

The small group walked down the hill, leaving Jeremiah to bury his mother, for no one could bear to see her covered with earth. As they walked down the hill, they heard the dirt being tossed into the grave. They walked close together, giving each other support. Malachi carried the old man's guitar. With his other hand he held the old man steady. Naomi walked with her arms around her children.

Back at the house, they sat on the porch in silence. Malachi wanted to wait for Jeremiah before he resumed his journey.

When Jeremiah returned, they said their goodbyes.

Malachi bent low and kissed Kathleen on her forehead. He shook hands with Noah. He got a kiss on the cheek from Naomi, and a strong bear hug from Jeremiah. The old man came up to Malachi and hugged him. Malachi felt the frail bones of the old man in his arms, and he knew it would not be long before he followed his beloved.

As he walked away, he turned and waved back every so often, till he could no longer see the little shack and the family that stood before it. He had mixed feelings. There was a heaviness in his heart, a heaviness he'd not felt in years, not since the death of his father. He felt sad, as if he was leaving home. He felt sorrowful, as if he had lost something. But he felt glad, as if he had gained something also. What that was, he didn't know; but he felt determined to find out.

Five

Dere Is Trouble All Over Dis World

It took more than two hours for Malachi to reach the spot where he and Noah met and turned back. He walked on for another mile, when he heard voices. He stopped to listen carefully. He heard sounds that made the hair on the back of his neck stand on edge. It was the sound of many men screaming in torment. It was as if the gates of hell opened, and the screech of tortured souls echoed throughout the forest. Scared but curious, Malachi followed it to its source.

Deep in the woods was a clearing; in the center was a large tent. That's where the shrieks came from. He'd seen such tents before as a soldier. It was a medical tent, a portable makeshift hospital.

As he got closer, he saw that it was a Yankee encampment. His first instinct was to turn and run. Then he remembered he no longer wore the uniform of a Johnny Reb. He was a preacher man.

"Halt, who goes there?" said one of two guards, pointing their rifles at him.

"My name is Reverend Jones. I was passing by and heard the shoutin'. I was wonderin' if I could be of some help."

"Tommy," the one solider said to the other, "go get the Colonel." He pushed the rifle at Malachi. "You can jus' stay put."

The other young soldier ran off, returning a minute later; an officer accompanied him.

"What do we have here?" asked the Colonel.

"My name is Malachi Jones, Reverend Malachi Jones. I was headin' east on the road down yonder, and I heard shoutin'. I came to see what it was. Now that I see, maybe I can be of some help."

"I'm Colonel Cutter. We can use any help offered. Tell me, sir, do you have any medical training?"

"I'm afraid I don't, Colonel."

"Well, we've got some soldiers facing the worst times of their lives here. They could use spiritual help, too. Please, follow me, sir."

Colonel Cutter was a large man with wide shoulders and large hands. His beard was dark and full, and his hair curly. One look in his eyes, you knew he was under incredible strain and had had little or no sleep for some time.

They walked towards the large tent. Colonel Cutter continued to talk. "Tell me, Reverend, do you have a strong stomach? I hope you don't scare easily."

"It's been a long war for all of us. I've seen my share," said Malachi.

Suddenly, it dawned on Malachi who these solders were. These were the few that survived the battle he'd witness only two days ago.

For some folks, the term "hell on earth" is exactly that…a term, a saying, a string of words. But sadly, for some it is a reality. Inside the large tent, there were rows of dozens of men on army cots, and just as many on blankets on the ground. There were two long tables. At each stood a surgeon dressed in a long white coat covered in blood, as were their hands and faces. On each table was a wounded soldier held down by other soldiers as the surgeons hacked off fingers, hands, feet, arms and legs. The cries of those in pain filled your ears. The only way anyone could hear you was to shout. The stench of blood that soaked the dirt under their feet into mud was putrid. The body parts that littered the ground rotted faster than the crew could take them outside and burn them. It was unbearable.

"Doctor, I've brought you some help," barked Colonel Cutter. "This is Reverend Jones."

"Do you have any medical skills?" bellowed the doctor, holding a blood-drench saw in his hand.

"No, I don't."

The doctor with wide, half-crazed eyes looked at the Colonel. "I've been standing in this same spot for two days, knee-deep in blood and body parts. And you know what's been going on in my mind. I've been praying to God for help. And what does he send me? Does he send me a nurse, a surgeon? No! Not even morphine or chloroform or even a bottle of ether. Instead, he does what he always does he sends a prophet with nothing but words." He looked at Malachi. "Sir, you are as useless as your god. Now, get out of my way. Go find some poor dying soul who wants to waste his last breath getting something off his chest, but just get out of my sight!"

Malachi began to back away when the young soldier lying on the surgeon's table broke lose of the medics holding him in place. He reached out, and grabbed hold of Malachi.

"Please, sir, don't let them take my leg, please!" the young man pleaded.

"Quick, grab him," the doctor ordered the medics who took hold of him again and held him down.

"Don't let them take my leg," the young man shouted at Malachi. "If they take my leg, I don't want to live. I don't want to live as half a man."

The doctor laughed at Malachi and spoke with strong sarcasm, "Go ahead, Reverend, you're a man of words. Why don't you give him some words of comfort, something to calm him down and accept his lot in life? Go ahead."

Malachi approached the young man, and placed his hand on his forehead. He gently brushed his hair back, cooling his brow. "What is your name, son?"

"Kenneth, sir."

"Kenneth, it hurts my heart to see this happen to ya. I wish it wasn't so. And I know it's goin' to be hard for ya. Nothin' like this is easy. And it grieves me to hear ya talk that a-way. But I understand." It was clear to all the young man was becoming calm. "Tell me, Kenneth, are ya man of God?"

"Yes I am, sir," the soldier replied softly.

"Well, I tell ya, a man of God is a man forever, with or without a leg."

"Will you pray for me, sir?"

"Of course I will, Kenneth, today and everyday of my life."

"Thank you, sir." The young man looked at the surgeon. "I'm ready, doctor. You may proceed."

The doctor looked into Malachi's eyes, "I'm sorry."

"Don't be," whispered Malachi, "I'm as surprised as ya are."

As Malachi maneuvered slowly about the tent, trying hard not to step on anyone, he fought to hold back the tears. Only a few days ago, he was a Confederate soldier. Were these his enemy? Surely not. They were men just like any other men he'd known. Only they had worn gray, and these men wore blue. Other than that, he couldn't see any difference. He had called them brother, then why not these men? Were they not his brothers, too? Then he remembered Marcellus told him he was a new creature. He was changing, and he knew it. He'd never thought or felt like this in his life. It was such a strange feeling to be moved to tears of sorrow, but to be filled with joy at the same time.

He spent time with as many of the wounded as he could. He asked them their names. He looked at the photographs of their families. He listened to their woes. He prayed with them. He wiped the tears from their eyes and held them as they died in his arms. When he got to the far end of the tent, he felt faint.

He wasn't sure if it was a dream or reality, but he heard singing coming from a few yards outside the tent.

Children, we shall be free
When the Lord shall appear

We want no cowards in our band
That will their colors fly
We call for valiant-hearted men
That are not afraid to die

We see the pilgrim as he lies
With glory in his soul
To heav'n he lifts his longing eyes
And bids this world adieu

Give ease to the sick, give sight to the blind
Enable the cripple to walk
He'll raise the dead from under the earth
And give the permission to walk

He followed the sound. In a clearing not far from the tent he found a small group of black men digging what were obviously graves. They were all dressed in Yankee uniforms, which surprised Malachi. When they stopped singing, they took notice of Malachi.

"Excuse us, sir. We didn't see you there," said one of the men.

"That's all right. Don't mind me. Ya just keep doin' what ya doin'," said Malachi.

"Oh, we can't stop," said another man. "We've been here two days tryin' to keep up with them doctors. But every time we get a hole dug, they bring two more out."

Another man stepped forward. "The idea is to bury 'em deep and then cover 'em up so no animals can get at 'em and eat 'em."

"What difference would it make?" said another. "The worms will get them sooner or later."

"That's different. That's natural. Not like some wolf or a bear nibblin' on your bones."

"Stop talkin' that way. You fellas are given me the creeps," said one of the men standing in a hole up to his chest, holding a shovel.

"No offense," said Malachi, "but I never knew the Union army had black soldiers."

"Oh yeah, there's plenty of us. They usually keep us all together, but war breaks up families, never mind companies. We're with the 103rd out of Boston."

"Boston!" Malachi exclaimed. "I used to tell people I was from Boston, but I'm really not," Malachi laughed.

The men did not get the gist of Malachi's personal joke.

"Black Union soldiers," Malachi said in amazement. "What made ya sign up?"

"Oh, we got more reasons to fight than most. We believe in the Union and in our people. It's still hard even in the north; but one day, the black man will be truly free…not just free, but equal."

"You're dreamin'," hollered one of the men.

"Of course, I'm dreamin'. If you don't dream, nothin' happens."

"Where's your church, Reverend?" one of the men asked.

"Ain't got one, I just go where the Lord leads me." After he said this, Malachi tried to remember where he'd heard the statement before.

"I never knew you could dig a hole in the ground by wagging your tongue. I always thought you needed a shovel." They all turned to see Colonel Cutter standing, watching, and listening with his arms folded.

They rushed back to work. One of the men spoke up. "Sorry, Colonel, we were only…"

"Only lollygagging," the Colonel finished for him.

"Please, sir, don't blame the men," Malachi said. "They only stopped to answer my questions."

"I know you mean well, Reverend Jones. But I ask you kindly to leave my men to their work. Time is of the essence, and we have such little of it before we must leave."

The men looked at one another wondering what he meant by having little time to prepare to leave. Not wanting the men to hear anymore than he wanted them to hear, he motioned for Malachi to step a few feet aside.

"It's too dangerous to remain here. The enemy is all around. We've overstayed our welcome. Much to the disapproval of my surgeons, we'll be taking up camp within the hour and taking these men up north. I'm sure many of them will die on the way, but I'm sure we'll all die if we remain. We have enough wagons to move them, and I'm sure we can find room for one more. If you would come with us, we could use the support."

Malachi looked to the ground, ashamed to look the Colonel in the face. "I'm sorry, sir; but I have important business to attend to southeast of here, not north."

"Southeast, but what's there?"

"I'm going to Shannon City."

"Shannon City; but there's nothing there, sir. All the plantations have been demolished; the city has been burned out. There's nothing there but an encampment where they hold Confederate prisoners and a small community of slaves who wander around aimlessly because their masters are all dead, and they have nowhere to go."

"It's of a personal nature, Colonel; I have to go."

"That's a shame. But I can't make you go. I only ask that you keep us in your prayers. Pray that we have safe passage and that we don't confront enemy."

"Colonel, I don't believe Confederate soldiers, seeing ya with so many wounded, would attack."

"You're a man of morals, Reverend Jones. This is war. There's no place for morals. If you don't kill your enemy when he's down, he may get back up and kill you."

Marcellus was right. Malachi was a new creature. There was a time he would have agreed with the Colonel. But now it made no sense to him.

"I will pray for your safe passage, Colonel."

"Thank you, Reverend."

"God bless you, Colonel, and your men."

The two men shook hands; Malachi headed off from the clearing and into the woods. He didn't want to pass the medical tent to return to the road he was on. He wanted to avoid it at all cost. He would come to the road sooner or later up ahead. As he became engulfed by trees, he could hear the shovels moving dirt behind him. He could hear the black Yankee soldiers from Boston singing as they toiled.

I've been 'buked an' I've been scorned, children
I've been 'buked an' I've been scorned
I've been talked about, sho's you're born

Dere is trouble all over dis world
Children, dere is trouble all over dis world

Ain't gwine to lay my 'ligion down

Children, ain't gwine to lay my 'ligion down

Six

My Soul Got Happy Dis Mornin'

Malachi saw a farmhouse a quarter mile up the road on his left. As he got closer, he could see a man behind a plow making furrows in a small plot of land next to the house. He was a short black man almost childlike in stature. He could barely hold the plow steady. What was most peculiar was neither an ox, nor mule, nor did horse pull the plow. Two large men with leather straps across their chests pulled the plow held by the little man across the field, first this way and then another.

When Malachi reached the field he leaned against the wooden fence watching. When the little man behind the ploy saw him he stopped. The two large men unstrapped themselves and went to a water bucket for a drink. The small man walked toward Malachi.

"Howdy," he cried. "You must be the new pastor."

"Excuse me?" said Malachi.

"Oh, forgive me. Where are my manners? My name is Percy Whittle. Those two beasts of burden are my sons, Jacob and Isaac." He called out to his sons, "Hey, boys come meet the new pastor." When they stood before Malachi, Percy made the introductions. "This here's Isaac, and this one's Jacob. I know what you're thinkin'. How did a runt like me father such big sons? Well, their mother's family was also on the large size. She was a good size woman, as women go. Big boned, ya might say, bigger than me, God rest her soul. But listen to me carryin' on like this. I didn't catch your name, Pastor…?"

"The name's Malachi Jones." Then Malachi pointed to the plow. "Why do ya use your sons to pull your plow?"

"Because, there ain't a beast within a hundred miles of here, first came the Rebels, than came the Yankees, then the Rebels again, and then the Yankees again. Every time, they'd take whatever they wanted till there ain't even a chicken in these parts. This land used to belong to the Wilson family. We were their slaves. But they're all dead now. Like most of the other plantation owners, dead or moved away. We slaves just stayed put, workin' the land. And we take care of each other real good."

"I've been travelin' hard," Malachi said. "I'm lookin' for a place called Shannon City."

"This here's Shannon City, or what's left of it," said Percy.

"Is there a Yankee encampment around here where they keep Confederate prisoners? I've got some business there."

"Sure is," said Percy, pointing down the road. "It's two miles into town, and the camp is five miles after. But I wouldn't go there, if I was ya."

"Why's that?"

51

"Because they ain't very trustin' souls. They sooner shoot ya than look at ya. They don't trust anybody, especially white folk, turned around collar or no. Besides, what ya need to go there for? The church is on the same road only a mile out of town."

"Percy, there seems to be some misunderstanding. You're referring to a church down the road, and ya keep callin' me Pastor. I don't know what you're talkin' 'bout."

"Well, Pastor Davis passed away…let's see, that's been two years this spring. When Pastor Davis passed away, before he died, he said they'd send a new pastor."

"Who is they?" Malachi asked.

"I don't know. The folks that send out new pastors when the old one dies, I guess. You're a man of the cloth. So, I put two and two together, and I figured ya was the new pastor."

"I'm afraid ya still have to wait. I'm just passin' through."

"That's a shame. The job's open, if ya want it."

"Thank ya, but no thank ya. Now, ya say the Yankees don't treat strangers kindly?"

"That's puttin' it mildly. I wouldn't go pokin' my nose around there, if I were ya."

"And ya say the church is just after the town and before the encampment. Does anybody live at the church now? I might stay there for a few days before I decide what to do."

"If ya need a place to stay, Reverend, ya welcome to stay with me and my boys. We got room."

"I appreciate that, but I need to be alone for awhile. Ya do understand?"

"Of course I do. If ya need anything, Reverend, ya know where to find us. Say your goodbyes to Reverend Jones, boys."

"Goodbye, Reverend Jones," his two sons said in unison with their husky voices.

Percy and his sons returned to their labor. Malachi returned to the road.

****

Malachi could see roofs of buildings over the tops of the pine trees up ahead. There was even a two-story building in the middle of town. As he walked down Main Street, all he heard was the sound of the wind howling through the empty buildings and broken windows. Shannon City was now a ghost town. Not a soul lived there. Many of the buildings were either burnt out or had been bombed out. There was not much left of them.

At the end of Main Street was the remnant of what must have been a fine-looking church. It had been bombed to the ground. The tip of its steeple lay at his feet. This surely wasn't the church Percy spoke of. Besides, he said it was on the road out of town.

He investigated a few of the buildings, the ones still standing, and found nothing. Both armies had pillaged properly. They'd taken everything of worth, especially food.

Malachi felt too lonely in such a desolate place to even take shelter for the night. He decided to press on.

The sky became dark. Malachi felt a few raindrops land on his head and heard thunder off in the distance. He would need to find shelter.

A Slave's Song

A mile or so from the town, he came on another church. This one wasn't as grand as the one he'd seen in town; but it was still standing. It was a typical country church, all whitewashed with green shutters on all the widows on both sides of the building. The steeple was small, but the bell was still intact. He walked up the six steps to the front double doors. He eased them open. They squealed and screeched for oil that no one applied for years. He entered just in time. The storm had arrived with full force. The rain came down hard, the wind howled, the lighting flashed, and the thunder cracked like the sound of cannons.

The inside of the church was dark and dusty. Cobwebs hung from the ceiling and clung to the walls. Some of the pews had been tipped over and were on their sides. The floorboards creaked under his weight. At the front was a tall pulpit, behind that was an organ, and behind that were the billows to work it. Behind the billows was a door. He had to force it open. It was too dark to see much. It seemed it was an office, and beyond that were living quarters. Malachi decided it too dangerous to venture further, so he remained in the church.

He found a large Bible resting in the pulpit. He blew the dust from off it, and gently opened it. From years exposed to all kinds of weather, it fell apart in his hands like the ashes of a burned log in a fire found cold in the morning. He stepped down and sat in the third row of the pews.

He was feeling low. The pounding rain was finding the weak spots in the roof and dripping all around. The lightning lit up the room, and then darkness flooded back in. The thunder shook the building.

He reached across the pew, taking hold of one of the hymnals in search of inspiration. Like the Bible, it too fell apart in his hands. The brittle pages flaked and dropped to the floor like a tree's dry leaves falling to the ground, till only a single page he held in his hand. He read it by the on and off flashes of lighting.

Can't you live humble?
Praise King Jesus
Can't you live humble?
To the dying lamb

Lightning flashes
Thunders rolls
Make me think
Of my poor soul

Everybody
Come here, please
See me, Jesus
On my knees
Come down here, and
Talk to me

Michael Edwin Q.

Went away, and
Let me free

The song frightened and comforted Malachi at the same time, such a strange thing to do. The rain leaking from the ceiling was not touching him. Tired beyond measure, he lay down on the pew, closed his eyes, and fell fast asleep.

****

Something woke Malachi. He sprung to his feet. He looked around. The morning light flooded the church. What woke him was the booming sound of the church organ. He looked passed the pulpit. Seated at the organ was an elderly black woman. Malachi could only see her profile whenever she shook her head to the sound of the music. Her fingers flew up and down the keyboard. She played a few bars to warm them up. Then she burst into song.

Good mornin', everybody
Good mornin' everybody, Lord
My soul got happy dis mornin'
My soul got happy dis mornin', Lord

Ya call me a hypocrite member
Ya call me a hypocrite member, Lord
But my soul got happy dis mornin'
But my soul got happy dis mornin', Lord

I'm gonna see my mother
I'm gonna see my mother, Lord
Gonna sit down by my Jesus
Gonna sit down by my Jesus, Lord

Good mornin', everybody
Good mornin', everybody, Lord
My soul got happy dis mornin'
My soul got happy dis mornin', Lord

She ended the song with a grand "Amen" played on the organ. Malachi didn't want to scare her, but he was so moved by her performance he put his hands together and applauded. It didn't scare her in the least. She turned around, saw Malachi, and smiled.

"Why, I didn't know I had an audience," she said sweetly.

"I couldn't think of a lovelier way to be wakened," Malachi said, still applauding.

"Why, that's most kindly of ya." She noticed his white collar. "Ya must be the new pastor."

"You're not the first person to ask me that. I'm sorry, but I'm not him. I'm afraid you're mistaken."

"You're a preacher, ain't ya?"

"Yes."

"And ya came here to Shannon City, didn't ya?"

"Yes."

"Well, if the good Lord took the trouble to make ya a preacher, and then He went out of His way to deliver ya here. Maybe you're the one who's mistaken."

Malachi thought it useless to push the notion, so he changed the subject. "And what is your name, dear lady?"

She turned from the keyboard and stood. She was a small woman...tiny to be precise. She'd done her long gray hair up in a bun. Her body and face was round, and her eyes squinted, giving the impression she constantly smiled. "My name's Addie...Addie Sims. And what is your name, Reverend?"

"Malachi...Malachi Jones."

Just then a small boy of perhaps five or six came from behind the organ. Malachi realized he was the one working the bellows.

Addie introduced him. "This here's Taint. Say hello to the new pastor, Taint."

"What kind of name is 'Taint'?" Malachi asked. "Is he your son?"

"Shoo, no. I ain't never even been married. Taint's not his real name. No one knows his real name. Everybody just calls him Taint. He Tain't mine, he Tain't yours, and he Tain't got a name."

"Nice to meet you, Taint."

The boy just smiled and nodded at Malachi.

"Oh, he don't talk none. He understands just fine, but he ain't said a word since his folks passed on."

"But the boy stays with ya, though?"

"Reverend Jones, maybe if I tell ya the story of Shannon City, you'd understand things better." She sat down again, facing him. "Shannon City was a quiet, peaceful Southern town, much like most towns. The main source of commerce was cotton from the plantations. As ya know, white folks owned these plantations; but we black folk, we slaves, worked them. Ya don't know what it's like to be a slave, do ya, Reverend? I hope not.

"See, most folk who don't know 'bout slavery think there are two types of Massa, one that treats ya good and the other that treats ya bad. A bad Massa works ya hard, feeds ya little, and beats ya when he pleases. A good Massa gives ya food, clothing, shelter, and Sundays off. At least that's the way a body who ain't never been a slave sees it.

"But a slave sees it for what it is. He sees it like God sees it, for what it truly is – a sin. Sure, it's better to have a Massa that treats ya decent. But that don't make him a good man. Good men don't own other men. It's just different levels of evil. Ya ain't got your freedom when you're a slave. And to have no freedom is liken to not havin' enough air to breath. Ya got this big sorrowful weight on your chest, always weighin' ya down, till one day it breaks your heart or kills your body, or both.

"Shannon City was that kind of place. Till the war broke out, that is. Most of the slave-owners are dead now, or their plantation has been so badly torn apart it can't be run no more. We slaves are left on our own to survive. Not free, just left to our own devices. Young Taint here is only one of the many children who ain't got anybody. Nobody can afford to take in another mouth to feed, so we share him. He stays with one family for a day or two, then another. This here's my week to take him.

"Now when the plantations failed, and we slaves were abandoned, Pastor Davis here at this church kept us goin'. He was our guiding light. But he was an old man, and one day he up and died. And we've been scattered ever since without a leader. That's why it's good ya came: we need a new Shepherd."

"Ya don't understand, Addie, I'm only here because I got friends in the Union encampment here."

Addie replied, "And what ya don't understand is that just because everything is quiet right now, this is still a war torn country. They ain't gonna let ya waltz in to no Union camp. I'll tell ya what, stay a few days at least; and I'll see if I can get ya into the camp. I got friends."

"I guess I can wait a couple of days," replied Malachi.

Addie stood again, took Taint's hand, and started for the front door. "Ya wait here, Reverend. I'll be back in a few hours with some food. Are ya hungry?"

"I could eat a horse."

"Sorry, all the horses been taken away by the soldiers: Yankee and Johnny Reb. Ya may just have to settle for parsnip soup."

"Sounds just fine," Malachi shouted to her as she was at the front door. "What should I do in the meantime?"

She shouted back from outside the church, "I don't know. What do pastors do when they're alone, ya tell me?"

Malachi heard their footsteps clobbering on the six wooden stairs, then along the gravel road, and then silence. He was alone.

****

Remembering Marcellus' advice, Malachi spent time reading his Bible, but eventually he became restless. He thought of leaving, but his stomach was empty and growling. The prospect of Addie returning with a hot meal was something he couldn't turn down.

Feeling a need to do something, Malachi explored the church hall. He found a broom closet. He took the broom and a shovel and began sweeping out the church. In no time, most of the floor he'd swept clean. He tried to straighten up the pews that lay on their side, but they were too heavy for one man to lift. Try as he may, though he grunted with exertion, he couldn't move them.

"What'cha doin', Pastor?"

The voice startled him. He stood up to see Percy Whittle and his two sons standing in the doorway.

"I was just tryin' to put these pews right," Malachi replied.

"That's no work for a man of the cloth," Percy said. He patted his sons on the back. "Boys, why don't ya two get those pews standin' right?"

The two strong, young men began lifting the pews up, putting them in their place. To Malachi's amazement, they did it swiftly and easily. Malachi got out of their way and went to stand by Percy. The two men watched in silence and awe at feats of strength that were beyond their capabilities.

Percy handed Malachi a sack. "Yams...just put `em in the fire for a few minutes, pull `em out and take off the burnt skin, and ya got dinner. I figured you'd be hungry."

"How'd ya know I'd be here?" Malachi asked.

Percy ignored the question and continued talking. "I got here as soon as I could. I don't like to be late, so I'm always early for everything."

Malachi gave him a questioning look. "Early for what?"

"For the meetin'."

"What meetin'?"

"The one Addie called. The others should be here soon."

"What others?"

"The rest of the community. We've been waitin' for a new pastor for a long time."

"Listen, Percy, there's been some misunderstanding."

"Don't tell me, Pastor, tell the others when they get here."

"And quit callin' me Pastor!"

"Whatever suits ya."

During the next hour, people arrived at the church: singles, couples, families. There were children running and playing outside. Inside, the young and old folks greeted one another like family. They came up to Malachi and introduced themselves. Everyone offered him food. Not large offerings; but added together, it made a sizable pantry-full. There were yams, potatoes, carrots, onions, bacon, eggs, flour, salt, and two loaves of fresh baked bread. After each introduction, the person smiled and told him how happy they were to meet him and how glad they were to have a new pastor. Malachi wanted to say something, but he couldn't bring himself to speak up. Finally, Addie showed up carrying a large metal pot.

"Here's the turnip soup I promised ya. It'll be good dunkin' for that bread I see ya got." She handed the pot to Malachi who placed it down with the other offerings. Addie got up and stood next to the pulpit.

"All right, all right. Everybody get seated and quit your gappin'."

It would seem Addie was not only the oldest person in room, but the spokesperson for the community.

She waited for all to be seated and hushed before she spoke. Malachi stood off to the other side of the room.

"Is God good?" shouted Addie. No answer. "I said, 'Is God good?'"

"Yes, He is!" random voices hollered back.

"And when is God good?" Addie went on.

"All the time," all the voices said together.

"Indeed," Addie said. "And we are blessed. We all know life is hard, but we're still standin'."

"Amen, sister!"

"We ain't free, but at least we ain't slaves anymore. So we're on our way!"

"Amen!" many voices hollered to the ceiling.

"And when ya think the Lord ain't listening, he comes across and answers your prayers. It gives my heart great pleasure tonight to introduce to ya our new pastor, Reverend Jones."

The entire congregation stood up, cheering and applauding.

Malachi took his place at the pulpit, holding his arms and hands up as if trying to hold back a river – it was useless. Finally, they went silent but remained standing, waiting to hear the first words from their new pastor.

Malachi put his hands down at his side and cleared his throat.

"Please be seated," he asked softly. They sat with smiles beaming at him. "I think there might be some misunderstanding." They remained smiling. He felt the weight of the task of telling them that he had no intention of being theirs or anyone else's pastor. He also felt it would be too cruel at that moment. Perhaps if he persuaded them to believe he wasn't the best man for the job, they'd change their minds. "What I'm trying to say is, I'm not really the best man for the job."

"No need to be so humble, Reverend," said Addie. "We know ya ain't perfect. We understand."

"That's not what I mean," Malachi said. "What I mean is…I've never been a pastor before."

"Don't worry, we'll break ya in," someone shouted from the back. They all laughed, even Malachi.

"And my studies," Malachi continued. "I wish I knew my Bible better. I don't know if I have what it takes to teach."

"Then we'll learn it with ya," someone else shouted. They all nodded their heads agreeing.

A middle-aged man seated with his wife and family stood up. "Excuse me, Reverend. My name is Abel Robinson, and this here's my wife Flora and the rest of my brood. Everybody here knows me, and I know everybody. So I'm sure they'll agree with what I have to say.

"Before the war, when the plantations were workin', we were slaves. We toiled night and day. Our lives were miserable. If it weren't for Pastor Davis and this here church, I don't think we would have survived. It became our heart, and we became family to one another. Now the war is almost over. The plantations are all gone, destroyed. And life ain't much better than it was. It's still a struggle; but at least I can see some light. But we're all scattered. We need to get together again, and help one another. I need my heart back, and I want my family back. We need this church to stay alive, and this church needs a pastor if it's gonna carry on. So I beg ya, to at least try. We will, if ya will."

Some folks were in tears. This moved Malachi's heart. "Perhaps we do it for awhile and see what happens."

They cheered and applauded, the smiles returning to their faces.

"But I have one more question to ask before I accept," Malachi announced. They went silent again. "I'm gonna be brutally honest, and I hope I don't offend anybody. But tell me now, or forever hold your peace." The air was heavy with anticipation. "If anybody has any qualms about ya all havin' a white pastor, say so now."

Percy Whittle stood up. "What color God do ya intend to preach, a white one or a black one?"

This took Malachi aback. "Why, I don't plan to preach no god of any color, black or white. The word of God is his word no matter what color is the man that preaches it."

"That's all I wanted to hear," said Percy. "I claim ya to be my pastor. All those in agreement say 'Amen'."

There were shouts of "Amen!" loud enough to shake the rafters.

A lanky young man stood up. His pockets were bulging with tools, hammers, nails, chisels, and a handsaw hung at his side from his belt. "My name is Woodrow Edgefield, but everybody calls me Woody because there ain't nobody in these parts that knows wood like I do. Now, I know a church is more than just a building; but that don't mean the building needs ignorin'. Just look around. This here place needs fixin' up."

"And you're just the guy to do it," Percy shouted. "All those in favor of makin' Woody foreman, say 'Amen'."

"Amen!" they replied as one.

"I'm honored by your confidence in me. I will do my best. We start tomorrow at dawn." Woody sat with the others.

Percy spoke loud and firm. "The Good Book says wherever two or more are gathered, He is there. Well, I look around, and I see a whole lot more than two. And I know we're gonna make it."

Malachi felt it a good time to dismiss everyone for the night. "Well, ya heard Woody. We'll meet here in the mornin'." It suddenly struck him that if he were to be a pastor, he'd need to start acting like one. "But before we go, let us share one word from the Good Book." He prayed a silent prayer the Spirit wouldn't fail him as he opened his Bible to a random page, pointed, and read out loud.

And let us consider how we may spur one another on
Towards love and good deeds
Let us not give up meeting together
As some are in the habit of doing
But let us encourage one another
And all the more as you see the Day approaching

Again, they let out a mighty *"Amen."* They all stood up. And when they did, Addie began to sing; and they all followed in song.

Children, go where I send thee
How will I send thee

I'm a-going to send thee
One by one
As the little baby born in Jerusalem
Two as Paul and Silas
Three as the Hebrew children
Four as the four who stood by the door
Five as the five Gospel preachers
Six as the six who never got fixed
Seven as the seven who went up to heaven
Eight as the eight who stood by the gates
Nine as the nine who never went behind
Ten as the Ten Commandments
Eleven as the eleven disciples
Twelve as the twelve apostles
Amen!

Slowly and silently, they left their pews and started filing out the door. Malachi remembering his pastoral duties, rushed to the front to shake each hand and thank them for coming and for their gifts, trying to remember as many names as he could.

The last to leave was Addie with one hand holding Taint's and the other holding a thick blanket.

"I praise the Lord for this day and for ya, Pastor Jones. Now I know you've had a full day, and I hate to bring this on ya, but I'm an old woman and I can only do so much." She placed Taint's tiny hand into his. "This is the last day for me to take care of Taint, so I'm leavin' him in your keepin'."

"But I thought y'all take turns takin' care of him?"

"We do, but this week is Ellery Thompson's turn, and he made a run for it up north. I pray to God he makes it. And every one else's hands are full. So ya see the poor child ain't got nowhere to go. Ya don't mind, do ya?"

"I guess it'll be all right."

She handed Malachi the blanket. "Here, he gets cold." She left the church and disappeared into the darkness.

Taint followed Malachi around the room as he blew out the flames in the hurricane lamps. Then he placed the child on the front pew, covering him with the blanket. He could see the boy's face clearly in the moonlight that broke through the windows. Sorrow and worry filled his eyes.

"Don't fret. Nothin''s gonna harm ya, I promise."

Malachi took out his mouth harp, blowing low and soft. After a few bars of *Barbara Allen*, Taint seemingly calmed down.

"Wasn't that nice?" Malachi asked as he finished playing. "I can teach ya to play, if you'd like." He handed the boy the mouth harp. "All ya gotta do is pucker your lips and blow."

Taint held the mouth harp with both hands, pressed it tightly to his chest, closed his eyes, and fell fast asleep.

Seven

Ain't Got Time to Die

Malachi woke in the morning to the sound of someone sawing wood. He checked on Taint who was fast asleep. Stepping outside to a world that still had one foot in the nighttime, he found Woody sawing on some lumber.

"Woody, what are ya doin'?" Malachi asked.

"Just wanted to get an early start; the others should be along soon."

Malachi wanted to complain, but how do you find fault in someone who is trying to make your life better? "I'll be inside. Would ya like something to eat?"

"I already ate."

Malachi just shook his head in disbelief and went back into the church. Sitting on the floor, being as quite as possible, he found a loaf of bread and tore the end off. Opening a jar of honey, he poured a few daubs onto the bread. He was just about to take a bite when he looked up to see Taint standing over him, staring at the piece of bread.

"Are ya hungry?" Malachi asked.

The boy just stared.

"Ya like bread and honey?"

The boy licked his lips.

"For what we are about to receive, may we be truly thankful," Malachi said as he handed the bread to Taint. He tore off another piece of bread and poured honey on it. The two sat on the floor, eating in silence. Just when they were almost finished, Percy walked in.

"Mornin', Pastor Jones," Percy said. "Looks like Woody got up before all of us. When did he get here?"

"Mornin', Percy. Let's just say there are roosters who were wakened by Woody's hammer and saw this mornin'." Malachi laughed.

"When you're ready, Pastor, folks are starting to show."

"I'll be right out."

After they finished eating and Malachi washed honey off Taint's face with some water from a jug someone had brought, he and the boy stepped out of the church into the morning light. Most of the folks were there now. They gathered as Woody gave them the itinerary.

"As y'all can see, the outer building is far worse than the inside. The inside just needs some cleanin' and a fresh coat of paint whereas the outside needs plenty of work. We need to replace some of the rotted wood, fix the roof, and give it some paint. I need the men to start tearing away everything that needs to be replaced. Ladies, if y'all can start mixin' paint, please."

They all scattered like a swarm of bees. Malachi took off his jacket and collar, placing them gently over a tree stump.

"Would ya like somethin' to eat, pastor?" asked one of the women holding a wicker basket. Malachi noticed all the women brought baskets, enough for lunch for all.

"Oh, no, thank ya. I've already ate," Malachi said. "But there is somethin' I'd like ya to do. Could ya keep an eye on Taint for me while I help the others?"

"Be glad to, Pastor."

Malachi's heart soared to new heights as he worked side by side with his new friends and flock. They gave of themselves freely and fully. Their joy was so great that they sang as they worked.

I keep so busy servin' de Lord
Keep so busy servin' de Lord
Ain't got time to die
'Cause when I'm givin' my all
I'm servin' de Lord
Ain't got time to die

They sung songs of the new found freedom they saw coming their way

No more auction block for me
No more, no more
No more auction block for me
Many thousands gone

No more peck of corn for me
No more driver's lash for me
No more pint of salt for me
No more hundred lashes for me
No more auction block for me
No more, no more

Many hands make light work, as they say, is indeed true. It was surprising how much work they completed in just the first few hours. Woody stood on a large rock and made an announcement.

"Everybody take a fifteen minute break. You're gonna need your strength. It's gonna start gettin' warm soon."

Everyone found a cool patch of grass to stretch out on. Malachi found Taint and took him by the hand, and the two sat down under a tree.

"I'm gonna teach ya how to play the mouth harp," Malachi said, handing the instrument to the young boy. "Ya gotta pucker your lips real small and blow. That's right. Not to hard, blow real gentle like."

After a few minutes, Malachi looked up to see a young man in his early twenties standing over them.

"The little fella sounds like he's gonna be a natural," said the young man.

"He does, don't he?" Malachi agreed. "He'll get good in time."

The young man stood tall and straight. "Pastor Jones, my name is Eli Johnson."

"Please to meet ya, Eli," Malachi said as he reached up and the two shook hands.

"Pastor, I was hopin' I could have a word with ya." He motioned toward young Taint. "Alone, if that be all right?"

Malachi rose and helped Taint to his feet. "Taint, why don't ya go show Addie how well ya can play mouth harp, while I talk to this young gentleman" The boy ran off, never taking his mouth off the harp.

"What's on your mind, Eli?"

"Same thing that's been on my mind for the past two years…Bessie Carter. That's her over there," Eli said, pointing her out.

"Nice lookin' girl ya got there."

"I think so, sir. We been courtin' for more than a year now. I asked her to marry me, and she said, 'Yes.' I built us a little place connected to where Percy Whittle lives. Ya know Percy Whittle? We'll, her folks and my folks have approved. In fact, everybody knows we're pledged."

"So, why haven't ya married the girl? What'cha been waitin' for?" Malachi asked.

"For a preacher, sir; and now that you're here, we can do it."

Malachi was taken aback at the thought, but he regained his composure quickly. "I suppose we can set a date."

"That's the problem, Pastor, we can't wait. We been waitin' so long. We hold hands when were alone, and I kissed her under the mistletoe last Christmas. We've been savin' ourselves. But now that you're here, I don't see why we need to wait anymore. I tell ya man-to-man, sometimes I look at Bessie and I think I'm gonna burst. If I hold it in any longer, pastor, I'm gonna die of heart failure."

"I doubt that," said Malachi. "You're a bit young for heart failure. But I guess we can do a wedding in a couple of days."

"No, sir, right now. We need to marry today."

"How does Bessie feel about this?"

"She's the one who sent me over here to speak with ya."

"And what do your folks say."

"They say they'er tired of watchin' us pinein' for each other all the time. They're in a hurry to get us out of the house."

Malachi thought for a moment. "Can ya at least wait for lunchtime?"

"I guess so."

"All right, we can have a weddin' at lunchtime."

"Halleluiah," shouted Eli. "Thank ya, Pastor Jones. I can't wait to tell Bessie." He ran off to tell his beloved.

Malachi walked over to Addie who was sitting on the grass next to the church with Taint.

"Addie, can ya do me a favor and watch Taint for awhile. I need to go and prepare for a weddin'."

"A weddin'?" she exclaimed. "My, ya do work fast. Who's the lucky girl?"

"Not me...Eli Johnson and Bettie Carter."

"Well, it's about time," Addie sighed. "When's the lucky day?"

"Today, at lunchtime."

"Lunchtime?" she cried out.

"I need to go into the church and prepare," he said.

"What's to prepare? Ain't ya ever did a weddin' before?"

He bent down and whispered to her. "To be honest, I never have. In fact, seein' how I never did, I thinkin' maybe I ain't got the right to marry anybody off."

"Ya can't marry anybody off," Addie agreed. "Only the Lord can marry two people. All ya can do is to facilitate."

"You're right," Malachi agreed. "Now, let me go and prepare for my facilitatin'. And spread the word. There's a weddin' at lunchtime."

Seated alone in the church, Malachi rattled his brains trying to remember how a wedding went. He'd been to a few in his day, from his cousin Teresa's wedding to when his Uncle Leonard remarried after twenty years of being a widower. But for the life of him, no matter how hard he thought, Malachi couldn't remember anything past "Dearly beloved." He opened his Bible and went into deep concentration. He didn't even notice that the hammering and sawing that went on outside stopped as folks prepared for the wedding.

As to how much time passed, he didn't know. When Malachi looked up from his Bible, and saw Addie and Taint standing in the doorway.

"Everything's ready. They're waiting for ya," she said.

"I'll be right there," he said. Addie and Taint left. Malachi took the pieces of paper he'd written notes on, placing them in the front of his Bible. He rose and left the church.

Outside, everyone had gathered into two groups, leaving an aisle down the middle between them. At the end of the aisle was a makeshift tressel of long, thin, bent tree branches. They'd woven wild flowers within the branches, and flower petals covered the aisle.

Malachi walked down the aisle to the tressel where Eli waited nervously. From behind a tree, Bessie appeared; one hand tucked into the crook of her father's arm, and the other holding a small bouquet of flowers. Everyone smiled and sighed as they walked down the aisle to the treacle. Looking at the father reminded Malachi about the tradition of giving the bride away, which he'd completely forgotten.

"Who gives this woman away?" Malachi asked, loud enough for all to hear.

"I do," said Bessie's father, Madison Carter, as he gave his daughter's hand to Eli.

Madison stepped back and stood with his wife, Casey. Bessie and Eli took their place before their pastor, Reverend Malachi Jones.

"Dearly beloved," That was the extent of Malachi's knowledge of a wedding ceremony. The rest would be from his notes and mostly improvisation. He opened his Bible, placing his finger on his notes. "We are gathered here today in the sight of God and friends to see these two get married proper." No one seemed to notice anything different, so he continued. Then he remembered something the minister said at his cousin Teresa's wedding. "If there's anybody who knows why these two should not be married, speak up." Folks looked at one another, but no one spoke up. After a proper wait, Malachi continued. "Marriage is important business, and ya must enter into it sober and serious."

The mothers' of the bride and groom began whimpering. Malachi waited for them to settle down.

"Of course, love is a big part of a marriage. Let's see what the Lord says about love:

Love is patient, love is kind
It does not envy, it does not boast, it is not proud
It does not dishonor others, it is not self-seeking
It is not easily angered; it keeps no record of wrongs
Love does not delight in evil but rejoices in truth
It always protects, always trust, always hopes, always perseveres

Not just the mothers were whimpering, now there were tears shed by many. Malachi continued to read from his notes.

Where you go, I will go
Where you stay, I will stay
Your people will be my people
Your God, my God
Where you die, I will die
And there I will be buried
May the Lord deal with me
Ever so severely
If even death separates you and me

Not wanting to press his luck, he decided to come to the end.

"Do ya have the ring?"

"No, pastor, we ain't got no rings."

"That's all right," said Malachi. "Rings ain't important."

Eli and Bessie let out a sigh of relief.

"Do you, Bessie Carter, take Eli Johnson to be your lawfully wedded husband and promise to be the best wife you can be?"

"I do."

"And do you, Eli Johnson, take Bessie Carter to be your lawfully wedded wife and promise to be the best husband you can be?"

"I do."

"Then I now pronounce ya man and wife. Ya may now kiss the bride."

Eli took Bessie in his arms and kissed her. The gathering burst into cheers and applause, and then with Addie taking the lead they broke into song.

> *This little light of mine*
> *I'm gonna let it shine*
> *Oh, this little light of mine*
> *I'm gonna let it shine*
> *Hallelujah*
> *This little light of mine*
> *I'm gonna let it shine*
> *Let it shine, let it shine*
>
> *All in my house*
> *I'm gonna let it shine*
> *Oh, all in my house*
> *I'm gonna let it shine*
> *Hallelujah*
> *All in my house*
> *I'm gonna let it shine*
> *Let it shine, let it shine, let it shine*

Again, cheers burst out as everyone crowded around the newlyweds to congratulate them.

Suddenly, the sound of gunfire cut through the air. Everyone stopped and listened. There it was again: gunshots off in the distance.

"It's comin' from the north valley," someone cried.

Malachi raised his hands to get everyone's attention. "I want the younger men to stay with the women and children. The older men come with me."

The group of older men ran off toward the sound of the gunshots to investigate.

Eight

I Once Was Lost

Malachi ran toward the sound of the gunfire with the small group of men behind him. They came to a ridge. The bursts of gunfire were loud enough to know they were coming from over the bluff. Malachi raised his arm to signal the others to halt. Then they continued up the hill slowly, keeping low to the ground. At the top of the ridge, they looked down on a clearing. There were no more than thirty soldiers…half Confederate, half Union…shooting at one another at close range.

Nearly every bullet found a mark. There was not one soldier who was not covered in blood.

"This is terrible," Malachi said. "We have to do something."

But they all knew there was nothing they could do but watch.

One by one, the soldiers fell dead. When they were out of bullets, they switched to hand-to-hand combat. Bayonets plunged into stomachs. Some picked up rocks and cracked their opponent's skull. Others fought rolling on the ground, choking each other. Finally, the fighting was down to four or five soldiers.

"Come on," said Malachi. "They've no more bullets, and there's only a few of them left. Let's stop this."

Lead by Malachi, they rushed down the hill. But when they made it to the clearing, only two soldiers, a Johnny Reb and a Yankee, were left alive, rolling on the ground trying to strangling each other. The men tore the two soldiers apart and held them. The two enemies spit and cursed. Malachi jumped between them.

"Stop it! Stop it!" shouted Malachi. "This is useless! The war is nearly over. There's no need to fight anymore. It's over!" The two men stopped struggling and began to calm down. "Let them go," Malachi said. The men holding the two soldiers looked at Malachi like they weren't sure they heard right. "Let them go," Malachi repeated.

The instant they were released, the Johnny Reb fell down, grabbed a handgun from a dead Union officer, rolled along the ground, got to his knees, pulling off two shots at the Yankee soldier. During the same moment, the Yankee soldier bent down, pulling a long knife from his boot and threw it underhanded at the Rebel. The blade flew, lodging into the neck of the Rebel, but not before the two gunshots landed squarely into his chest. Both soldiers were dead before they hit the ground.

The small group stood staring at all the dead, feeling hopeless.

Malachi looked to one of his companions, "Go back to the church. Tell the women to remain there with the children and do whatever they can to clean the church. Tell the other men to bring some shovels and picks. The repairs on the church will have to wait. We have graves to dig."

They lined the bodies in rows, not caring to separate Confederates from Union soldiers. No one bothered to search through pockets or backpacks for anything of worth. That felt too disrespectful.

When the other men arrived with the shovels and picks, they started to dig the graves. The men sang softly as they worked.

The Lord, He thought He'd make a man
These bones gonna rise again
Made outta mud and a handful of sand
These bones gonna rise again

I know it
Indeed I know it, brother
I know it
These bones gonna rise again

It was early evening; the sun was dipping into the horizon when they had nearly all the bodies in the ground and covered with earth. The women and children appeared at the top of the ridge. They waved and came down to meet the men folk. They carried the baskets of food that were planned for lunchtime.

"We figured y'all must be thirsty and hungry, so we brought ya somethin'," Addie told Malachi.

The men took a break, sitting on the ground, eating and drinking. There was a silence over the clearing that was uncomfortable, to say the least. Even the children remained quiet. As they ate, Malachi gathered all the rifles and pistols. He emptied them of bullets and placed them in a pile. He found some dry kindling, and placed it between the weapons. He struck a match and lit the kindling. The flames grew higher; eventually the rifles caught fire. Everyone couldn't help but gaze into the fire as they ate. When they finished eating, they returned to the task at hand. When they'd covered the last grave, Malachi felt it was time to say something, a time to pray.

"Were these truly enemies? Brothers dressed in gray and blue. Brothers with different views, views so strong they felt it worth killing and dying for. Well, now they have killed, and now they have died, and there's no one left. No one really wins a war, and there has never been an end to it.

"Heavenly Father, have mercy on the souls of these brave men, forgive them for their shortcomings and take them to your bosom. Amen."

"Amen," everyone echoed.

One of the women stepped forward and began to sing; the others followed.

Free at last, free at last
I thank God I'm free at last
Free at last, free at last

I thank God I'm free at last

Ways down yonder in the graveyard walk
I thank God I'm free at last
Me and Jesus gonna meet and talk
I thank God I'm free at last

On my knees when the light passes by
I thank God I'm free at last
Thought my soul would rise and fly
I thank God I'm free at last

Some of these mornings, bright and fair
I thank God I'm free at last
Gonna meet King Jesus in the air
I thank God I'm free at last

When the fire died out, Malachi started up the hill, the others followed. Not a word was spoken, and no one looked back.

****

It only took a few more days to get the outside of the church looking fine. After they cleaned the worship hall and repainted it, they did what repairs they could to the pump organ, to the delight of Addie who regained her place as head of the music ministry.

What was difficult was cleaning the living quarters behind the pulpit and the organ. Not only because years of neglect had left the rooms in disarray with dust and cobwebs, but because the memories each person had of Pastor Davis made them tarry in their work.

The first room was a small office with barely enough room for the desk and an extra chair. There were dozens of books on shelves on the walls and above the desk. Papers were sprawled over the floor and desktop. Malachi rummaged through the desk drawers. It seemed Pastor Davis had not only saved his sermons but categorized them under different topics and kept a drawer for sermons for all the major Christian holidays. The large drawers to the right and left of the desk were filled with them. It relieved Malachi to know he'd not be lost for words on any given Sunday.

Beyond the office was a short and slender hallway, just large enough for one person at a time to pass. The walls were cabinets filled with more books and Pastor Davis's writings, a theological university's worth of information at Malachi's fingertips. At the end of the hallway were three steps leading down to the kitchen. It, too, was a small room made smaller by the table and chairs and a large, black, iron cast stove, which took days to clean and restore to working order. There were three doors along the kitchen wall: the right and left were two small bedrooms; the center door opened to the outside world. It wasn't much, but it was more home than Malachi had had for many years.

That first day, after all the repairs were done, and Malachi and Taint moved into the back rooms, everyone said their goodbyes and wished them well. Addie stayed late to prepare them their first meal in their new home, red beans and cornbread.

"Why don't ya stay and have dinner with us?" Malachi suggested to Addie.

"Nah, ya two need to get settled in your new home," said Addie. "Besides, tomorrow is Sunday, your first service in our renewed church. Ya must be excited."

"I guess so," Malachi said, inwardly feeling very apprehensive of facing the dawn.

Malachi left Taint in the kitchen. The boy was using a spoon to break up his cornbread in the deep bowl of red beans, as Malachi walked Addie outside.

"Addie, who is it who's next on the list to take care of Taint?"

"I don't rightly know. I have to check and see."

"Well, I was thinkin'. It ain't right for a child to be passed 'round like a hot potato. Maybe it would be best if he just stays with me for now. Besides, he's gettin' real good on the mouth harp; it'd be a shame to stop his musical lessons just now."

"Yeah, it would be a shame," Addie said with a smile. "Right now, the two of ya might be just what the other one needs." Addie walked off into the darkness. "See ya in church, Pastor. We're all lookin' forward to your first sermon."

"Yeah, so am I," Malachi mumbled under his breath. "Good night, Addie," he cried into the darkness.

Back inside, he found Taint asleep, his head down on the kitchen table. Malachi picked him up, brought him into his room, gently placing him on his bed. Careful not to wake him, Malachi took off the boy's shoes and covered him with the blanket. He was just leaving when he noticed something clutched in the boy's hand, something shiny. It was the mouth harp. Malachi bent low, kissing the boy on his forehead.

Malachi lit the hurricane lamp in the office and began looking through the desk's drawers. He took a pile of papers out, placing them on the desk.

"There's gotta be a good sermon in here somewhere," Malachi sighed. "Lord, if you're lookin' down on me now, please don't laugh, though I wouldn't blame ya if ya did. But I sure could use your help, please."

****

Taint worked the bellows as Addie played the organ. The folks stood singing, though poorly, for they were distracted looking about the church, admiring their own handiwork. Finally, after the third hymn, they all concentrated on what they were doing and sang like angels sent from heaven. Malachi was nervous, concentrating on his notes, dreading the moment the music would stop – and then it did.

Everyone sat, remaining silent, waiting for Malachi at the pulpit to speak. He cleared his throat three or four times, and then he began his sermon.

"What words should I speak to ya today? What words would make ya happy, more believin', more thankful, and more lovin'. What words would bring ya closer to God, make ya a better person, and stronger in your walk?" Then he held up his Bible. "What words can I say that ain't been said already? Ya wanna be happy?" He opened his Bible.

"Delight yourself in the Lord and he will give you the desires of your heart.

"Ya need more believin'?

'If you have faith as small as a mustard seed, you can say to the mountain, "Move", and it will move. Nothing will be impossible for you.'

"Ya wanna be more thankful?

'For everything God created is good, and nothing is to be rejected if received in Thanksgiving.'

"Ya wanna get closer to God?

'Draw near to God and He will draw near to you.'

"Are ya tryin' to be a better person? Just look to one another.

'Iron sharpens iron, and one man sharpens another.'

"And ya wanna know about Love? The Lord has lots to say about Love. It's His favorite subject.

"'Do onto others as you would have them do to you. – Love your enemies, and then your reward will be great. – Love sincerely. Cling to what is good. – Love your neighbor as yourself. – Love is the fulfillment of the law. – Faith, hope and love, but the greatest of these is Love. – Love covers a multitude of sins. – Everyone who loves is born of God and knows him. – We love because he loved us first. – Love binds everything in perfect unity. – Whoever does not love does not know God. – For God so loved the world that he gave His only Son that who believes in Him shall not die but have eternal life.'

"And that's just to name a few. If ya need a miracle, then just look around, look at the fine work y'all did to rebuild this church. Look at your children, strong and healthy and livin' in hope. Look to yourselves, close as any family, takin' care of one another, and gettin' through the most dangerous times this here land has ever known.

A Slave's Song

"We are all truly blessed. And I thank God for all of ya. Please, stand up and let us sing 'Amazin' Grace.' Addie, if ya please."

As Taint began pumping the bellows, Addie played on the organ; and all the folks stood and sung so loud and so hard the rafters shook.

Amazin' grace! How sweet the sound that saved a wretch like me
I once was lost, but now I'm found, was blind, but now I see

`Twas grace that taught my heart to fear, and grace my fears relieved
How precious did that grace appear the hour I first believed

The Lord has promised good to me; His word my hope secures
He will my shield and portion be as long as life endures

Yes, when this flesh and heart shall fail and mortal life shall cease
I shall possess, within the veil, a life of joy and peace

The earth shall soon dissolve like snow, the sun forbear to shine
But God, who called me here below, will be forever mine

When we've been there ten thousand years, bright shining as the sun
We've no less days to sing God's praise than when we first begun

When the last note faded, Malachi smiled at the congregation; and they smiled back.

"Thank y'all for comin'. I pray God gives y'all a fine week. And all God's children said...?"

"Amen!" they conclude.

Malachi rushed to the front of the church to say goodbye to each and everyone. But instead of receiving handshakes and smiles, he was met with hugs and tears of joy. They were now a church.

Nine

It's Good Enough for Me

Time did what time does; it passes so slowly, and is gone so quickly. The church and its community flourished. Addie formed a church choir. There were men's Bible study classes, and women's classes, and Sunday school for the children. Best of all, they looked out for one another's welfare by helping, feeding, visiting, and working for and with one another. Malachi continued to study all the notes and books Pastor Davis had left. And Taint grew taller and became proficient on the mouth harp.

Amid all this, Malachi did not forget his true reason for coming to Shannon City. The thought of his comrades imprisoned at the Yankee camp never left him. If there was a way of helping them escape, he'd do it, even to the death. But he needed to know the situation. Yet, how was he to do this? Many times folks warned him how distrusting the Yankees were of strangers, especially white folk. Then it dawned on him. The idea came to him one morning. He packed a lunch for two, and he and Taint headed down the road toward the Yankee camp.

They saw the camp from a quarter mile away. It was in a large clearing. There were long wooden barracks. It was easy to tell which ones they used to house the prisoners. Those barracks were surrounded by high barbed wire fences with so many thick strands it would take an hour to cut through. There was an armed guard at each corner of the fence.

Malachi waited and watched for a long time till he saw someone stand by the fence, wearing a Confederate uniform...someone he recognized. It was Corporal Dewitt and two of the privates from his company.

Malachi scribbled a message on a scrap of paper and handed it to Taint.

"Ya see those men over there, behind the fence? I want ya to take this message and give it to them. Can ya do that for me?" Taint nodded. "Good boy. Be careful and come right back."

Taint walked out in the open, nonchalantly. The guards saw him, but paid him no mind. What harm could a small black boy do?

Standing at the barbwire fence, Taint looked at the three soldiers.

"What's the matter, son, ya lost?" Dewitt asked.

Taint held his arm out, holding the scrap of paper.

"Sorry, son, if you're lookin' for a handout, ya came to the wrong place," said Dewitt. "We get barely enough food to live on ourselves."

Taint refused to move and continued holding out his arm.

"I told ya we ain't got nothin' here for ya, so ya might as well go home. Ya do have a home, don't ya, son?"

A Slave's Song

Taint put the message in his shirt pocket. He reached into his pant's pocket, pulling out Malachi's mouth harp, and he began to play. It took Dewitt and the other two by surprise. It wasn't so much that such a small boy could play so well, it was the song he played – *Barbara Allen* – and the way he played it. Clearly, it was a style they were familiar with, even though they hadn't heard this rendition in quite a while.

"Where did ya learn to play that song?" Dewitt asked, moving closer to the fence.

Taint stopped playing and pointed his thumb over his shoulders to the woods behind him.

Dewitt looked at one corner of the fence. The Yankee guard was rolling a cigarette. He looked to the other corner where that guard was staring into the horizon in his boredom. Dewitt took hold of the bottom strand of barbwire and lifted it high enough for Taint to slip in under the fence. It was too low for a grown man, but Taint had no trouble.

"That was great harp playin'. Come on in, son. I'd like my friends to hear your playin'. They won't believe it."

The barracks were long, lined on both sides with army cots. In the middle of the room was a stove the men used for heat at night and to make coffee during the day. At the front of the room were tables for eating and playing cards. When they weren't on work detail, the prisoners would stretch their legs on the small confined grounds allowed them, or spent their time together in the barracks passing the long hours in conversation. The Union soldiers treated them fairly. They never mistreated them, the food was tolerable and adequate; but there was no denying it, they were in a prison camp.

Dewitt entered the barracks carrying Taint under one arm like a sack of potatoes.

"What'cha got there, Dewitt, an enlisted Yankee soldier?" one of the men hollered.

"What soldier? It's probably a Yankee General, from the size of `em," spouted another.

"Maybe it's a secret weapon," laughed another.

They all walked to the front of the room, laughing. Dewitt stood Taint on top of one of the tables.

Captain Malory pushed his way to the front. He looked at Taint and then at Dewitt, and smiled. "Who's your new friend, Dewitt?"

"Captain, ya gonna fall over when ya hear what this young fella can do." Dewitt smiled at Taint. "Go ahead, son, show `em what ya showed me."

Taint reached into his pocket, took out his mouth harp, put it to his lips and began to play. The men backed off in silence, amazed. He only played one verse, but it was enough to get the point across.

"That's just the way Malachi used to play it," stated Sergeant Hastings.

Captain Malory laughed. "Hastings, you're tone-deaf; and even you heard the similarity. There's somethin' goin' on here, and we need to find out what." He moved close to Taint and spoke softly. "What's your name, sonny?"

Taint stood silent and motionless.

"Maybe he's deaf," Private Roland said.

"How could he be deaf? He just played the mouth harp," replied Corporal Hood.

"Don't be afraid, sonny. What's your name?" Malory asked again.

Taint reached into his shirt pocket and handed the scrap of paper to the Captain.

"It seems our suspicions were right. This letter here's from your friend and mine, Private Malachi Jones. It says, 'Hey boys, I ain't dead. I'm alive, and I ain't far off. Tell me how I can help. Yours truly, Malachi Jones'."

Captain Malory found a pencil and paper on one of the other tables. He scribbled a quick message, folded the paper, and handed it to Taint.

"Here ya go, sonny. Take this to the man who gave ya the note. Will ya do that for me?"

Taint nodded the affirmative.

"Dewitt, see that he gets out of here safely," Malory ordered.

"One minute, sir," Corporal Hood said. "Let him play just one more song." Hood smiled at Taint. "Do ya know any other songs?" Taint smiled. "Well then, let's hear it."

Taint began to play. After just a few bars, the men recognized the song; and they all began to sing.

Give me that ole time religion
Give me that ole time religion
Give me that ole time religion
It's good enough for me

It was good enough for the Hebrew children
It was good enough for the Hebrew children
It was good enough for the Hebrew children
And it's good enough for me

It will bring you out of bondage
It will bring you out of bondage
It will bring you out of bondage
And it's good enough for me

It will do when the world's on fire
It will do when the world's on fire
It will do when the world's on fire
And it's good enough for me

Their voices grew louder. Their spirits soared. They crooked their arms together and dance in a circle as they sang.

"Hush up, the guards coming," shouted the man at watch at the window.

The room went silent. Captain Malory took hold of Taint, and put him on one of the cots. Malory placed his finger over his lips to hush the child, and drew the covers over the boy's head.

"What in blazes is goin' on here?" shouted the Union soldier as he ran in holding his rifle.

Captain Malory stepped forward. "We're just tryin' to lift our spirits in song, sir."

"I thought I heard a harmonica," said the guard.

"That's Corporal Dewitt, here," replied the Captain. "He kind of squeaks when he sings." All the men laughed.

"Well, keep it down before the commanding officer hears ya. This ain't Christmas, ya know," the guard grumbled as he left.

Captain Malory went to the cot, grabbed Taint, and returned him to his place atop of the table.

"You've got the note. I need ya to give it the man ya came with," Malory said.

"Hold on," said Corporal Hood. "We can't let the boy go without knowin' his name."

"But he don't speak," insisted the Captain.

"Then let's give him a name," said Hood, taking off his cap, holding it out to the others. "Everybody write a name on a slip of paper, and we'll have a drawing to see what his name is."

Everyone passed paper and pencils around, writing out their favorite name and placing it in the hat.

"This is stupid," said Hastings.

"Ya wouldn't think it so stupid if ya didn't have a name," Hood replied.

He swirled the pieces of paper around in his cap. He pulled a name out, and read it slowly.

"Well, what does it say?" the Captain asked.

"Seems we got a joker in the pack," said Hood. "Somebody didn't write down a name. They ripped a piece out of their Bible and put it in my cap."

"Well, what's it say?"

"It's from the book of Matthew, chapter one, verse twenty-three. It says, *Behold, a virgin shall be with child, and shall bring forth a son, and they shall call his name Emmanuel, which being interpreted is, God with us*."

"Then Emmanuel it is," said the Captain, writing it down on a slip of paper. "From now on your name is Emmanuel," he said as he handed the boy the folded paper. Again, the Captain looked at Dewitt. "See that he gets away safely."

"Come on, Emmanuel," said Dewitt taking the boy by the hand. He walked him out and up to the fence. Dewitt held the barbwire up. The boy ducked under and out.

"Hey, you, stop!" shouted one of the guards as he ran toward the child.

The newly christened Emmanuel ran, fell, picked himself up, and scampered away.

"Ya wouldn't shoot a little black boy in the back, would ya, Sergeant?" Dewitt hollered at the guard.

It was true; he didn't even take aim at the boy.

"What was he doin' here?" the guard asked Dewitt.

"Lookin' for food, ya know how it is."

Emmanuel ducked into the woods. He ran till he was met by Malachi.

"Hold on, hold on," Malachi said as he took hold of the boy, who was out of breath. "Are ya all right? Did ya get my message to my friends?" Emmanuel nodded. Malachi continued his questioning. "Did they give ya a message for me?"

He reached into his shirt pocket and handed Malachi a slip of paper.

At this point, we need to have a good understanding of the workings of a child's mind. To a child, a treasure is something that you hold close, like in your shirt pocket. Something important, like the message from Captain Malory, must be held in the hand at all times. This explains how the child had dropped the captain's note when he fell.

Malachi unfolded the message and read it out loud, "My name is Emmanuel."

****

The walk home was slower and longer. It was nearly dark when they returned to the church. Four saddled horses were grazing out front. Seated on the steps of the church were four white men dressed in western wear. When Malachi and Emmanuel approached, the eldest of the four stood to greet him, the others followed his lead.

"Good evening, Reverend Jones, we finally meet," said the man.

There was an uncomfortable feeling in the air. Malachi bent down to Emmanuel. "Go in and wash-up for dinner."

Trying to avoid touching the men, Emmanuel rushed into the church.

"How do ya know my name?" Malachi asked.

"Word gets `round, it's a small community."

"And who are you?" Malachi asked, first looking to the man and then at the others.

"My name's Jack Bates. But what's important is not just to know who I am, but who I used to be...who we all used to be," Jack said, pointing to the men at his side. "We represent a committee of landowners in the area. I used to own the biggest plantation in these here parts. The war's pretty much shut us down for now. Nothin' grows on our land, our slaves are all scattered, and we ain't doin' much better than they are. Of course, when the war is over and the Yankees leave, things will return to normal. Till then, we just do what we can.

"Now, we know ya been pastor here for these colored folk for awhile; and we think that's a good thing. In fact, when Pastor Davis built this church, I gave him my blessing. I know religion gives a body hope and a reason for livin'. Ya can't control a slave if he believes he's got nothin' to gain and nothin' to lose."

"What are ya tryin' to say?" Malachi asked bluntly.

Jack laughed. "I see you're a no-nonsense kind a man, just like me. Well then, I'll come right to the point. We men of the landowners committee...and there's quit a few more of us...have decided to rebuild the church downtown, and we'd like ya to be our pastor."

"I already have a church," Malachi said.

"We know that, and we want ya to keep over this here church. But ya can also pastor our church."

"Like I said, 'I already have a church.' If ya folks want to be a part of it, you're welcome. But I don't go downtown in the mornin' and preach a white god and then come here in the afternoon and preach a black god. There is only one God, and he's everybody's God. Now if y'all excuse me, I got a supper to cook." He walked up the steps of the church. He was just about to enter when Jack grabbed him by the sleeve.

"Listen preacher. I'm a reasonable man. I'd give ya the shirt off my back, if you're on my side. But ya don't want to know what I do to folks who ain't on my side. Don't get on my wrong side, preacher; it ain't a good place to be. Now, I know in time you'll come to your senses, so I'm gonna give ya some time to think about it."

"My answer will still be the same," Malachi snapped back.

"We'll see," Jack said, stepping down and walking away, the other men following. They mounted their horses. Jack admired the one large tree on the property. It was full and green, with one very large branch some twelve feet from the ground. "I see this tree is still doin' well. I'm glad," Jack said. "Ya know what we call this tree around here? We call it the *Hangin' Tree*. We hung many a man from that there very branch." He looked down at Malachi. "This here tree is a lot like your God. It don't care if a black man hangs from it or a white one. Ya have a pleasant evenin', Reverend Jones."

He dug his heels into the side of his horse. The group galloped away. Malachi watched as they rode off. When he could no longer hear the scamper of hooves, he walked back down the stairs and stared at the large tree then he stood under the one large branch and looked up and quoted scripture.

He will away every tear from their eyes
And death shall be no more
Neither shall there be mourning
Nor crying, nor pain anymore
For the former things have passed away

"But until that day, Lord, give me strength." Malachi said as he entered the church, wondering what he would make for dinner.

Ten

If Ya Get There Before I Do

It was late one Friday night. After putting Emmanuel to bed, Malachi settled behind the desk in the church office. He thumbed through Pastor Davis's notes, trying to select a sermon for Sunday's service. He pulled the right-hand lower drawer out as far as it would go. That's when he found it, a notebook bound in leather. He opened it to the first page. It was Pastor Davis's day-to-day journal. Starting at the beginning, skipping pages every so often, he began to read.

February 9, 1858

I cannot say for certain when the hunger to do the Lord's work came over me; nor can I say who or what instilled it within me. I only know it was put there by the Lord to come to this moment and this place. The plantation owners have given me their blessing. Their hope is that I sooth their slaves into submission with religion. I may have my church only if I preach from the Bible and not try to stir anything up. I suspect they're not well-read in the Good Book. The Lord's word isn't made to do much else but to stir people into action.

The slave community here is made up of good people, and they're excited about having a church. There is a young man named Woody. They call him that because of his fondness for working with wood. He even carries a handsaw at his side at all times. He has the know-how for raising a church and is determined to having the community construct it in less than one month.

Then there's Percy who lives very close to here. He has two strong sons and a lovely wife. He seems to be a man of Biblical and worldly wisdom as well.
A saintly woman named Addie. She has true musical talent and I know she will be a blessing to the church choir.

There's a young man named Buckley. The other young men look up to him. He is a true leader, if only I can get him to lead the others in the right direction. But he is not happy being a slave, and I don't blame him. But he is hot headed and does not know how to bite his tongue. I fear he may do more harm than good.

As for the others in out little community, I am slowly getting to where I can remember their names. They are committed to making this church a success.

****

March 19, 1858

Halleluiah, the church is complete! Except for a few finishing touches, we will have our first service next Sunday. I am so proud of these folk. They truly put their all behind this project, thanks to the direction of Woody who truly lived up to his name.

To my surprise, Jack Bates, one of the richest plantation owners in the area and a leader to the other owners, came by for a visit today. With him were two of his foremen driving a wagon with a large crate in the back. It was an organ for the church, which he'd ordered all the way from Chicago. I thanked him for his donation. But I understand why he's done this. He wants me to feel in his debt that I might keep my congregation...all the slaves in the county...well-behaved, especially the misbehaving Buckley and his followers. He felt his investment well-spent when I assured him I would not preach anything that was in disagreement with the Bible. Obviously, the man was not familiar with the story of Moses or the book of Exodus: "let my people go."

****

March 21, 1858

Today was our first service. It was spectacular. It warmed my heart to see each and every one in attendance. They sang like angels; and true to her word, Addie guided them through the hymns like a captain at the helm of a schooner. My sermon was on new beginnings, which I felt was appropriate.

After service, we gathered on the grounds for a barbecue picnic. I brought up the point that our little church didn't have a name. All agreed to just call it "The Church," as everyone felt a no-frills, no-nonsense approach was better. Besides, when you said "The Church" everyone knew what you were talking about.

Malachi shuffled a few pages forward.

June 4, 1859

Oh, happy day! We have just had our first wedding here at our little church. The marriage was between Lilly Reeves and Woodrow Edgefield, the groom better known as Woody. We held the service late in the evening so as many folks as possible could attend after working on the plantations all day. The reception was potluck, and singing and dancing went on into the night.

I do want to bring up this one point, though it really is of no consequence. As I have mentioned sometime ago, Woody earned his nickname from his love of working with wood. I have never met a man as talented as he in woodwork, nor have I ever met a person so happy in his chosen field. But when he stood beside his lovely bride during the ceremony, both of them dressed in their finest clothes, to see him still with his handsaw dangling from his side gave me pause. Enough said.

Malachi thumbed further into the pages.

September 18, 1860

To everything there is a season. Today we have had our first death, our first funeral. Millie Whittle, the wife of Percy Whittle. She had been sick for months. I visited her on many occasions during her illness. As she grew worse, she became resolved in her death. In time, there was nothing I could tell her. She knew she was dying and was prepared to do so. She would miss loving family and friends, but she accepted the will of the Lord with a smile. I can only hope that when my time comes I can muster such faith.

The church was packed to the rafters to see Millie off proper. There wasn't a dry eye to be found. Percy and her sons seemed to take it well, but I know them, in their deepest of hearts they were crying. We have a small plot of land behind the church we have designated for a cemetery. Millie Whittle is the first. And knowing life, she will only be the first of many. It was at the gravesite that Percy and the boys finally broke down and shed their tears. So many of us all did, too. She was a good woman and will be missed. We gathered around the grave and sung a hymn as we laid her in the ground.

> *Before I'd be a slave*
> *I'd be buried in my grave*
> *And go home to my Lord*
> *And be saved*
>
> *Oh, what preachin'!*
> *Oh, what preachin'!*
> *Oh, what preachin' over me, over me*
>
> *Oh, what mourning over me, over me*

A Slave's Song

Oh, what singin' over me, over me
Oh, what shoutin' over me, over me
Oh, weepin' Mary over me, over me
Doubtin' Thomas over me, over me
Oh, what sighin' over me, over me
Oh, freedom! Over me, over me

More pages on.

July 16, 1861

The months of rumors are now confirmed true. There is war! This country has been torn asunder, North against South, brother against brother. Some say it is being fought for political reasons, others say for moral ones, such as the abolishment of slavery. Either way, the future of the slave in this country is in the balance. It is in God's hands.

Jack Bates, the leader of the landowners, has visited to express his concern for my cooperation in these matters. The landowners feel that in these troubled times, their grip on their slaves must be tighter. For they fear rebellion. I, too, have misgivings, but for different reasons. The young men of this parish have always spoken up against slavery, here in the church. I have never tried to stifle them, as I agree with most of what they say. But I do fear their methods may do more harm than good.

****

August 24, 1861

I've met with Buckley Thomas, a handsome young lad. The other young men of the parish look up to him, and many swear allegiance to him. He has always spoken against slavery to all who would listen. He's even spoken of rebellion. I tried to persuade him to stop such talk, as the landowners still have much power, and any action against them now could be detrimental to our community. I begged him to be patient and to wait on the Lord.

The Lord is never slow, he is always on time. But to a young man who thirsts for freedom, God's timing is far too sluggish for his taste. The other young men are the same as he, impatient. An with the sound of Union gunfire off in the distance, Buckley has become bolder. I rear the worst.

****

Michael Edwin Q.

November 12, 1861

I am writing this from my bed. I have told those who have visited me in the past two days that I am simply under the weather. Many folks have been kind enough to bring hot meals, so I can remain in bed to recuperate.

True, I am not well; but my affliction is manmade. I received a visit two nights ago from the landowners committee, led by Jack Bates. They were not happy with the way the slaves, especially the young men, were acting. The war between the North and South instilled hope in the slave, and the landowners did not approve. I would even go so far as to say they feared it.

To drive home their intent, they dragged me from the church, tied me to the large tree out front. They tore my shirt off my back, and with a bullwhip gave me a dozen lashes. I realize they let me off easy, for they didn't want to incapacitate me, which would sway me from the task they wanted me to perform – to sway the folk of our church to keep the status quo.

So here I lay in bed, waiting on the Lord's healing hand. I dare not tell anyone the truth, as I fear the reaction from some of our hotheaded young men may put all in danger.

****

December 20, 1861

This is the saddest day of my life. All my efforts to try to keep the peace has failed and all my pleading to keep enduring for the time being has fallen on young deaf ears.

I was wakened this morning by the sound of horses riding off. I went out to investigate. Everything seemed normal, till I looked at the large tree in the front of the church. There, hanging from the limb was a limp body, a rope around his neck. I rushed back inside and got a knife from the kitchen. I ran out and cut the rope that was tied to the trunk of the tree. I rushed to the body lying on the ground and turned it over. It was Buckley. I barely recognized him; his face was so battered and bloody. I was too late; he was dead.

The word of his death traveled throughout the countryside. The other young men, friends of Buckley, gathered together. Using whatever they could get their hands on… farm tools, kitchen knives…they set out to take revenge on the landowners for their lost friend. They didn't get far. They were gunned down on the road as they marched.

Six young men shot dead and one hung makes for many funerals. I'm afraid any sounds of joy that might have been heard this Christmas will be drowned out by the sound of crying and wailing. I also fear this may not be the last of it.

****

May 2, 1862

This area has been occupied by the Confederates, then the Union, and then the Confederates again. And I'm sure at some point the Union will return to take their turn as king of the hill. At first, the fighting took place in the valleys on the far end of the county. We could hear the cannon and gunfire throughout the day. As weeks went by, the rumble became closer till they were among us. They fought in the town; they fought on the farms and on the plantations. Eventually, what the landowners feared came to pass. Their land was war torn, rendered useless. They lost nearly all control of their slaves. Their old way of life seems destine for extinction.

They came to me, to blame me. They said I'd lost control of my people. They never understood that I never had control; I never wanted it; and if I had, I would have spoken against them. Instead, I spoke only the word of the Lord; and it was that which convicted them.

But I must admit I fear them for they are like wounded beasts, ready to snap at whatever comes near. And the folks in our church have been slaves all their lives. This glimmer of hope of a coming freedom has made them more rebellious and daring. They help the Union soldiers when they can. They sabotage where and when they can. When they run from the plantations, it has become too costly and bothersome to hunt them down. In time, they will ignore the landowners, and they will do and live as they please and there will be nothing the landowners can do. But I fear the landowners will not give up without a fight. I see no alternative to bloodshed.

****

August 28, 1862

Jack Bates and the other landowners have given me an ultimatum – get my people under control or else. They still don't understand I do not and will not tell my congregation to submit any longer. I preach against violence, but I speak of freedom. As Saint Paul said, "Once you have made a stand, keep standing."

The landowners will never understand my relationship with these fine people. Their demands I can never meet. I have lived too long, and seen too much suffering. The Lord will tolerate so much, and vengeance will be his, not ours. I say, "Stay strong, my brethren, fight the good fight, run the good race, and all will be well in the end." I say this because I can see the end if I squint hard enough. I know my end will not be an easy or graceful one. Perhaps, I will dance the dance of death for a brief moment from the tree I see from this very window. But I fear no evil, for my Lord is with me. His rod and his staff, they comfort me, and I will dwell in the house of the Lord forever. A new day is dawning, so I sing.

*Pure city
Babylon's fallin' to rise no more
Oh, Babylon's fallin', fallin', fallin'
Babylon's fallin to rise no more*

*Oh, Jesus, tell ya once before
Babylon's fallin' to rise no more
To go in peace an' sin no more
Babylon's fallin' to rise no more*

*If ya get there before I do
Babylon's fallin to rise no more
Tell all my friends I'm comin', too*

Malachi slammed the book closed and put it back in the desk where he found it. He went in to check on Emmanuel, and found him deep in sleep. He left the church and started up the road. When he got to Percy Whittle's place, he stepped up onto the porch and pounded on the front door. Percy answered the door half asleep and yawning.

"Pastor Jones, what wrong?"

"Why didn't anybody tell me they killed Pastor Davis? They hung him on that big tree in front of the church, didn't they?"

Percy hesitated for a moment. "We was afraid ya might leave."

"Ya could have at least given me the benefit of the doubt," said Malachi.

"Well, I wouldn't worry too much about it. It's doubtful they'll kill one of their own," said Percy.

"Is that what ya think? That I'm one of them?"

Tears began to well up in Percy's eyes. "No I don't, and I'm sorry I said that. I just meant they might not kill a white man."

"As far as they're concerned, I'm no longer white." Malachi turned and started toward the road. "And as far as I'm concerned, I couldn't care less."

"Then ya ain't gonna leave us, Pastor Jones?"

"Not on your life."

Eleven

Like a Tree Planted by the Water

Malachi stepped up to the pulpit to give his Sunday sermon. Before he could utter a word, the sound of horses' hooves in a gallop filled the air. Everyone looked out the windows. It was the landowners, led by Jack Bates. They stopped just under the big tree. Only Jack dismounted. They heard his boots on the church stairs. He swung the front doors open, and walked in. The room went quiet as he slowly walked to the front of the room. He stood below Malachi, in front of the pulpit. He tuned to face the crowd, and placed his hands on his hips.

"As ya can see, I ain't wearin' any gun. I didn't come here to cause ya no harm or trouble. I just wanna say a few things. We've been through a lot together. And whether or not ya like it or ya refuse to believe it, one day the Yankees are gonna leave this county. Win or lose, the Yankees are gonna be gone, and everything is gonna be like it was. It's just the nature of things. Now we can do it the easy way, or we can do this the hard way. You've had your fun; now be realistic. Don't make it hard on yourselves.

"First thing we need to do is rebuild the church in the town. Pastor Jones will still do services here, but he can also do the one in town."

Jack's eyes searched the crowd till he found Woody. "Woody, we're gonna need your help with rebuildin' the church."

Malachi interrupted, "Mr. Bates, I already told ya this town already has a church."

"Let the man answer his own questions," snapped Jack. He turned to Woody, again. "What'd ya say, Woody, will ya help us?"

Woody stood up. "I'm sorry, sir, but I'm standin' with my pastor."

"You'll live to regret that, Woody," Jack said, pointing his finger at Woody. He spun around toward Addie. "Addie, didn't I give ya that church organ?"

"This is a house of God, Mr. Bates, sir. I thought ya gave it to God," Addie said.

Jack spun around again and started pointing out different individuals. "Tessie, when ya were havin' a hard time deliverin' your first child, ya nearly died. Didn't I call the doctor around for ya? Marvin, when your mother was dyin', didn't I let ya go without work for two days, so ya could be by her side? Woody, didn't I buy ya all the wood-workin' tools ya wanted, included that there handsaw? I was never one for usin' the whip unless a body deserved it, and y'all know it. Didn't y'all have a roof over your heads; and wasn't there always food in the pot, meat sometime's, too? Not like now, y'all strugglin' to stay outta the rain, listenin' to your stomachs growl. One day the Yankees will be gone, and things will be like they were. Now we can do this friendly like, startin' right now. Or we can do it later, and it won't be friendly."

A Slave's Song

Percy Whittle stood and addressed Jack to his face. "None of us here know their heritage, where they came from, or what their true name would have been if they were born there. All of that was taken away from us and can never be returned to us. Ya make threats as if death were the worst thing that could happen to a person. There have been times in many of our lives where death would have been a blessing.

"True, the last few months have been a struggle, but all our life has been a struggle. But we have enjoyed an independence, a freedom, we have never known, and it is the most gratifying thing we posses. Ya tell us that one day things will return to the way they were. That will never happen. We would die first. So, go on and make your threats. What can ya do to us that hasn't already been done? This is God's house so I'll be as kind as I can. Ya no longer have any power over us. Ya have no power here, Mr. Bates, so would ya please leave."

"Y'all be sorry!" Jack shouted, pointing at them. "I'll be back, and the next time it ain't gonna be friendly. I gave y'all a chance, and this is how ya repay me. Me and the others will be back and then..."

Just then, Addie pressed down on the organ keyboard, drowning out Jack Bates' threats. The congregation stood and began to sing.

When Israel was in Egypt's land
Let my people go
Oppressed so hard they could not stand
Let my people go

Go down Moses
Way down in Egypt land
Tell ole Pharaoh
"Let my people go"

"Thus spoke the Lord," bold Moses said
"Let my people go
If not I'll smite your first born dead"
Let my people go

No more in bondage shall they toil
Let my people go
Let them come out with Egypt's spoil
Let my people go

Jack stormed out of the church in anger. He mounted his horse and rode off with the other landowners at his side. As they galloped away, they could hear the congregation singing.

Michael Edwin Q.

I shall not be moved
Like a tree planted by the water
I shall not be moved

When my burden is heavy
If my friends forsake me
Don't let the world deceive you
I shall not be moved

****

Malachi found three hymnals which were in poor shape, nearly falling apart and put them in an old sack. He took Emmanuel to Addie's home for her to watch over him while he was gone for the day. He slung the sack over his shoulder and headed down the road to the Yankee camp.

As he approached the entrance to the camp, two armed guards pointed their rifles at him.

"Halt! Stay right there, Mister. State your business," said one of the guards.

Malachi stepped forward, and in his best northern accent said, "I'm Reverend Jones, pastor at the church in Shannon City. I'd like to speak with your commanding officer."

Never taking his aim off Malachi, the one soldier ordered the other, "Go see if the Colonel wants company. You just stay right there, Reverend."

The soldier slung his rifle over his shoulder, entered the camp, and ran off to what looked to be the main building. He returned a few minutes later.

"Colonel says bring him in," said the returning soldier.

"What's in the bag, Reverend?"

"Just some old hymnals I thought the prisoners might like," Malachi said, opening the sack and letting the guard take a look.

They opened the fence; Malachi followed the one soldier onto the compound. They entered the larger building and walked down the hall to a door. The Soldier knocked.

"Come in," a muffled voice seeped through the door.

A tall and stout Union officer greeted Malachi when he entered the office. His eyes and his hair were dark, as were his sideburns, which were long, standing out a good three inches from his face. The officer reached across his desk to shake hands with Malachi.

"Pleasure to meet you. Reverend Jones, wasn't it? Please, have a seat." The officer sat down also. "My name is Colonel Collingsworth. My guard tells me you're the pastor at the church at Shannon City. I thought that building was destroyed."

"The community rebuilt it," Malachi said, not wanting to go into details and let the captain believe they were talking about the same church.

"I recognize your accent, Reverend. You're from Boston aren't you?"

"I am," said Malachi. "How did you distinguish what city so quickly?"

"I've got family in Boston. What part of the city are you from?"

Malachi silently wondered if every northerner was either from Boston or was related to someone in that city. Malachi didn't know any more about Boston than he knew about the moon. He changed the subject quickly, placing the sack on the captain's desk. "I have some hymnals here I'd like to share with your prisoners. I'm sure being captive could wear on a man's spirit."

"That's very kind of you, Reverend. I'll see that they get them," Colonel Collingsworth said as he took hold of the sack.

"I'd rather deliver them myself," Malachi said. "I might be able to be of comfort to them."

"I suppose that can be arranged," the Colonel said, handing the sack back to Malachi. "Reverend Jones, I must tell you the truth. I have an ulterior motive for seeing you today. Not long ago, a little black boy was seen sneaking out of the camp. I believe the boy is the liaison between the prisoners and some Confederate spy in the area."

"How do you know that?" Malachi asked.

"Because the boy dropped this, a note," he said, holding up a slip of paper. "Tell me, Reverend Jones, do you know everyone in Shannon City?"

"Mostly everyone. Why?"

"Do you know anyone named Malachi?" he asked, as Malachi opened the note.

Malachi,

It was so good to learn you are still alive. We've missed you. It is good to know we have a friend on the outside. We have no plans of escape. But now that we know you are near, things may change. Do nothing at this time. Stay in touch.

Malory

"Who is this Malory?" Malachi asked.

"Captain Malory, the head officer over the prisoners here. You'll get to meet him when you deliver the hymnals. But what I need to know is, do you know this Malachi fellow? He certainly lives near by. He might even be one of your congregants."

"I really couldn't say," Malachi said, not wanting to say. "But I'll keep it in mind."

"Well, if you hear of anyone going by that name, let me know. As well, when you give the prisoner's the hymnals, see what you can learn. Try to gain their confidence. Maybe you can visit them again sometime. I'd appreciate any help I can get."

Malachi returned the note, and holding the sack, he stood up. "I understand, Colonel. I'll see what I can do."

"Thank you, Reverend. I'll have one of my men escort you to the prisoner's barracks."

****

All eyes went wide and jaws dropped when Malachi entered the prisoner's barracks accompanied by one of the guards.

"That will be all, Sergeant. I can take it from here. I'd like to be left alone with the prisoners." Malachi said.

"You sure you want to be left alone with this lot?" remarked the guard.

"I'll be just fine, thank you," Malachi said.

The guard left, everyone stood still and silent till they were sure he was gone. When they were, they rushed Malachi, patting him on the back. Captain Malory pushed them aside and stood before Malachi.

Looking him up and down, he laughed, "There's got to be a dilly of a story behind that getup. Malachi, where have ya been?"

"That's Reverend Jones, to y'all. In fact, don't even mention the name Malachi. Seems your Captain Collingsworth found your note ya tried to get to me. He even asked me if I know anyone named Malachi."

They all broke into laughter.

Malachi continued, "It's a long and crazy story, but the folks in this region think I'm a preacher."

"How'd ya get Collingsworth to let ya in?" Malory asked.

"He wants me to gain your confidence and spy on ya. Maybe y'all try to escape now that ya got a friend on the outside of the name of Malachi."

There was more laughter.

Malachi handed the sack to Captain Malory. "Here, these are some hymnals I brought ya. That's the excuse as to why I'm here that I gave Collingsworth."

Captain Malory handed the sack to Dewitt.

Malachi continued, "Collingsworth says I can visit y'all anytime I want so I can spy on ya. I can get food and clothing. Is there anything y'all need?"

"Forget all that," Malory said. "Is there a way ya can help us escape?"

The smile left Malachi's face. "I don't know. Maybe I can and maybe I can't. I do know one thing; I don't think I wanna help ya."

The smiles left their faces.

"What are ya sayin'?" asked Malory.

"I'm sayin' is that things have changed, Captain. I've changed."

"Changed? You're still a soldier, Jones."

"I'm a soldier all right. But Captain, I've changed armies. I no longer believe in North and South, blue and gray. I'm in the army of the Lord, now. I'm tired of war and I'm tired of fightin'."

"You're actually takin' that get up seriously?" the captain asked.

"It ain't the clothes, Captain. It's me. I've got friends on the outside. I can get ya out of here. I can help ya escape, but only on one condition." He hesitated a moment. "Ya got to promise me y'all just go home and forget killin'."

"We can't do that, Malachi. We're still soldiers," Malory replied.

"Why can't we?" Corporal Hood interrupted. Everyone turned to look at him. "We all know the war is over. The South has lost. The horse is dead, and I don't wanna risk my life tryin' to escape so I can go beat it some more. And I certainly don't wanna kill for a lost cause, and I definitely don't wanna die for one. I say we cut our losses, get out of this prison, and go home."

"Does anyone else feel this way?" The captain asked. He looked around to see their heads nodding. "All right, all those who want to call it quits, raise your hand." Every hand went up. He looked to Malachi. "Well, it would seem in one fell swoop you've made us all civilians again." He presented himself to Malachi. "But we won't get far in these gray uniforms. If ya and your friends can get us outta here, we're gonna need some new clothes."

"I'll talk it over with my friends and get back to ya once we have a plan," Malachi said.

"The guard's comin'!" shouted the watch.

"Everybody act natural," the captain ordered. "Our lives are in your hands, Malachi, Godspeed."

"Time's up, Reverend," the guard announced as he entered the barracks.

"Thank you, Sergeant. We'll be just one more minute," Malachi said, and then he addressed the men. "Enjoy the hymnals and use them in good heath. I'll be back in a few weeks to see how you are all doing. Let us end this day by singing. Open your hymnals to page eighty-five."

Gonna lay down my sword and shield
Down by the riverside
Gonna lay down my sword and shield
Down by the riverside
Ain't gonna study war no more

Gonna put on my long white robe
Down by the riverside
Gonna put on my long white robe
Down by the riverside
Ain't gonna study war no more

Gonna talk with the Prince of Peace
Down by the riverside
Gonna talk with the Prince of Peace
Down by the riverside
Ain't gonna study war no more

Twelve

An' Why Not Every Man

"I appreciate ya invitin' us to supper here at the church, Pastor Jones," Addie said. "But what I want to know is why jus' us three: Percy, Woody, and me?"

They were all seated at the small table in the living quarters of the church. They had just finished eating. Malachi placed his hand on Emmanuel's shoulder. "Why don't ya go outside and play, son. I'll call ya when we cut the pie."

Emmanuel scampered out the backdoor. They could hear him off in the distance playing his mouth harp. A solemn look came over Malachi's face.

"I've asked ya three here because I need a favor, and I can't think of anyone in our church who I feel confident in speakin' about it or any others who can make my request come true.

"Ya know ya can depend on us, Pastor," Percy said.

Malachi took his time before speaking, trying to put his thoughts in order. "I wasn't always a preacher. I used to be a soldier, a Confederate soldier."

There was a look of surprise on their faces.

"I'm sorry I hid this from ya. I didn't think it would matter, but it does now."

"No it don't," Addie said. "It don't matter at all. It don't matter what'cha did, what matters is what ya does now. Heck, Pastor Davis was a dentist before he came south and started this here church; and he was a good man and preacher. And so are ya. Ya been a good preacher and a good pastor, and that's all that counts."

The others nodded their heads in agreement.

"But what the Confederacy stands for, and its views on slavery," Malachi insisted.

Addie reached across the table, placing her hand on Malachi's "Listen, all the men of God had their pasts that they had to leave behind and live down. Abraham laughed at God; Jacob lied to his father; Moses was a murder; David was an adulterer, and Peter, who ate and slept with the Lord, denied Him three times. But they all rose up, dusted themselves off, and became great men of the Bible. I'm lookin' at my pastor today, not yesterday. Now put that behind ya, and tell us what's on your mind."

Malachi cleared his throat. "The men I soldiered with are in a prison camp…"

"The one that's just south of here?" Woody asked.

"Yeah, that's the one. I went to visit them. They've asked me to help them escape. At first, I told them no; but when they swore if they were free they'd give up soldierin'. That's when I told them I would."

Percy sat up straight, tilting his head. "Pastor, you're askin' for us to help ya?"

"Yes."

"You're askin' a small group of black slaves to help a company of Johnny Rebs escape from a prison camp?"

"Yes."

"Why not?" said Woody. "They said they'd give up soldierin'. It'd be the only Christian thing to do."

"Ya gotta promise no one gets hurt, Yankee or Rebel," Addie demanded.

"I agree," Malachi said. "That's where ya three come in. Percy, ya got a fine mind. If anyone could figure a plan to get them out without anyone gettin' hurt, it would be ya. Woody, I never known a body who could work so well with his hands to make things happen."

"What about me?" Addie asked.

"Addie, ya got a way with folks. If anyone can get them to help, it'd be ya." Malachi rose, walked to the stove, grabbed the pie and a knife, placing it in front of them on the table. "Think about it. Sleep on it. Tomorrow, after church, we're all goin' down to the river for some baptizin'. We can talk about it after." Malachi went to the backdoor to call Emmanuel. "Did I tell ya, Emmanuel wants to be baptized tomorrow?"

"How do ya know?" Woody asked. "Did he tell ya?"

"Don't need words. We got our own way of communicating." Malachi shouted out the backdoor. "Emmanuel, come and get some pie!"

****

There was an air of anticipation that day during Sunday service. The idea that they soon would be by the riverside for the baptisms filled them with excitement. Riverside baptisms meant celebration, a barbecue lunch, games, swimming, a day of fun. The children could not contain themselves. They squirmed in their seats like ants were crawling over them. Malachi went through the motions of giving a sermon. The adults went through the motions of listening to a sermon. When he realized how futile his efforts were, Malachi cut his sermon short and dismissed the congregation. They met outside and walked together down to the river, singing as they went.

> *The Gospel train's comin'*
> *I hear it just at hand*
> *I hear the car wheels rumblin'*
> *And rollin' thro' the land*
>
> *Get on board, little children*
> *Get on board*
> *Get on board, little children*
> *There's room for many more*
>
> *I hear the train a-comin'*

She's comin' round the curve
She's loosened all the steam and brakes
And strainin' every nerve

The fare is cheap and all can go
The rich and poor are there
No second class aboard this train
No difference in the fare

At the riverside, they got right down to business, the baptisms being the most important part of the day. Malachi took off his jacket and slowly waded out into the water. One by one, the faithful, men, women, and children, went out to meet Malachi to be baptized. The last to be baptized was Emmanuel. The boy pinched his nose as Malachi dunked him under. When he rose, the strangest of things happened.

"Praise be!" Emmanuel shouted to the sky.

Everyone stopped what they were doing, silently stared at the child. Malachi smiled at Emmanuel.

"My name is Emmanuel," said the boy.

Malachi wrapped his arms tightly around Emmanuel, holding him to his breast.

"Papa," Emmanuel whispered.

Malachi let him go; as he passed each person he said their name. "Addie, Woody, Tessie, Jenny, Percy..."

"It's a miracle," someone hollered.

Everyone was in tears. Addie took a long cloth she brought just for the occasion and wrapped it around Emmanuel.

Suddenly, like a black cloud that appears, blocking out the sun, their joy was tossed asunder, when they heard the sound of horse hooves. The landowners galloped up to the water's edge. There were more of them than before. This time they came armed.

Jack Bates was at the front of the pack. Still mounted, his hand resting on the hilt of his gun, he looked at all present. "I hope y'all thought over what I said the last time we met. We landowners thought it over and decided the day of bein' a nice fella is over." He pointed at Woody. "I want ya and your people to start work on rebuildin' the church downtown tomorrow. I don't wanna hear no stories or excuses. I want everybody there, ya hear? Ya know how hard I can be, Woody. Don't make me do somethin' harsh. Y'all be there." He took his gun out of his holster and pointed it a Malachi. "And preacher man, ya gonna stop bein' so uppity, and do what you're told, or I swear I'll shoot ya. No, I won't kill ya, because I want ya to preach at the new church. But don't misunderstand me. I may not kill ya, but I sure can make ya wish ya were dead." He put his gun back in his holster, and looked again at Woody. "Tomorrow at first light."

Everyone watched with their mouths gapping as the band road away. They silently walked from the shoreline to a nearby clearing. The men gathered large piece of dead wood and made a campfire for the ones who'd been baptized to sit by and warm their bones. No one prepared any food; no one felt hungry anymore. As the sun went down, all around them grew dark, making the light from the orange flames seem all the brighter. Feeling the joy of the day had been sucked away like marrow from a bone. They silently stared into the fire, till Addie began to sing. They all joined in.

Nobody knows de trouble I've had
Nobody knows but Jesus
Nobody knows de trouble I've had
Glory, hallelujah

One mornin' I was a-walkin' down
Oh yes, Lord
I saw some berries a-hangin' down
Oh yes, Lord

I picked de berry and sucked de juice
Oh yes, Lord
Just as sweet as the honey in de comb
Oh yes, Lord

Sometimes I'm up, sometimes I'm down
Oh yes, Lord
Sometimes I'm almost on de ground
Oh yes, Lord

What make ole Satan hate me so
Oh yes, Lord
Because he got me once and he let me go
Oh yes, Lord

Nobody know de trouble I've had
Nobody know but Jesus
Nobody knows de trouble I've had
Glory, hallelujah

Some of the men took buckets, went down to the river, bringing back water. They doused the fire out, till they all sat in darkness. Without a word, they rose and started for home. Malachi took Emmanuel's hand; they walked back to the church.

****

Malachi entered Emmanuel's bedroom to tuck him in. He sat down on the edge of the bed, gently brushing the child's forehead.

"Did ya say your prayers?" Malachi asked.

Emmanuel shook his head.

"Ya know, Emmanuel, I was so happy to hear ya talk today. I'm so proud of ya."

Emmanuel just smiled up at him.

"Since ya started talkin', ya can talk anytime ya want to." Emmanuel remained silent, smiling. "I guess you're gonna be a slow starter. We'll just take it slow, a little bit every day."

Malachi stood up, leaned over the hurricane lantern, blowing out the flame. Walking through the dark room to the light of the kitchen, then Malachi stood in the doorway.

"Goodnight, Emmanuel," Malachi said, before shutting the door.

"Goodnight, Papa," he heard Emmanuel say before the door closed.

There were so many feelings stirring in him – mixed feelings. On one hand, he was so happy and grateful that Emmanuel found his voice. On the other hand, what had happened with the landowners was tearing him apart. He felt ashamed. He should have said something. He should have stood up to them, guns or not. He'd let down his congregation – his friends. Worst of all, he felt he'd let down God. If he was to be a man of the cloth, he should act like one. Not standing up for what is right is not the Christian way. He felt a coward.

He sat down at the desk in the office, digging out Pastor Davis's journal. He was a wise man. Surely there was something written in it by the sage of Shannon City that would comfort and strengthen him. Toward the end of the book, he found a short passage that spoke to his heart.

I'm so afraid of the landowners and their threats. But why, what can they do to me? Does not the Good Book tell us?

What shall we then say to these things? If God be for us, who can be against us?

I should have stood up to the landowners long ago. Come what may, I will fight them tooth and nail. When my heart is in fear, he is with me. And so I sing.

> *He delivered Daniel from de lion's den*
> *Jonah from de belly of de whale*
> *An' de Hebrew Chillun from de fiery furnace*
> *An' why not every man*

> *De moon run down in a purple stream*
> *De sun forbear to shine*

A Slave's Song

An' every star disappear
King Jesus shall-a be mine
De win' blows east, an' de win' blows west
It blows like a judgment day
An' every poor sinner dat never did pray
Will be glad to pray on dat day

Can't ya see it comin'
Can't ya see it comin'

Didn't my Lord deliver Daniel
Deliver Daniel, deliver Daniel
Didn't my lord deliver Daniel
An' why not every man

Malachi closed the book and held it to his chest. At that moment, it became so clear. He knew what he had to do.

Thirteen

I Am Free

It was dark when Malachi woke. He went into the kitchen, prepared breakfast, and then laid it on the table. He quietly entered Emmanuel's room. The light from the kitchen shown on the boy's face, making him squint and then turn over. Malachi stood over him and shook him gently.

"Wake up, sleepyhead. It's gonna be a busy day. I made tatters with your eggs the way ya like `em."

Slowly rubbing his eyes, Emmanuel got out of bed, washed his face in the basin, and put on his clothes.

Seated at the kitchen table, Malachi said grace, poured himself some black coffee, watching Emmanuel eat his breakfast.

"I'm dropping ya off to spend the day with Addie. I'm goin' to be busy most of the day. I'll pick ya up later tonight."

"Addie," said Emmanuel with his mouth full.

"Well, one word a day is better than none," Malachi said, sipping his coffee.

****

Addie's home was a short walk from the church. It was a one-room shack she'd lived in for thirty years. It had a covered front porch with holes in the floorboards. From the porch, you could see the steeple of the church above the treetops. Addie sat on the porch in her old, dilapidated rocking chair.

"I was hopin' you'd watch Emmanuel today, while I go on some business," Malachi said.

"Course I will. The little darlin's a pleasure to be with. Come here, child."

"Addie," Emmanuel said as he ran into her arms.

"That seems to be the word for today," Malachi said.

"Well, that's one word more than usual," Addie replied.

"My sentiments, exactly."

Emmanuel sat on the surface of the porch and reached down into one of the holes.

"Oh, don't do that, child. There ain't nothing but snakes down there." Emmanuel pulled his hand back out. "Go inside, child, go get ya one of the apples on the table and bring Addie one, too. That's a good baby."

When they were alone, Addie looked down and smiled at Malachi.

"Who ya kiddin' with that 'I got business to attend to' malarkey," Addie said. "Ya goin' downtown to do your duty, and get our folks outta there."

"Ya say it's my duty, like I'm doin' somethin' smart," Malachi groaned.

"Well, the smart thing ain't always the right thing, and the right thing ain't always the smart thing. But I tell ya, the right thing is always the right thing. Somebody's got to stand up to them landowners."

"Like Pastor Davis?"

"Like I said, it don't have to be smart to be right."

Just then Emmanuel came out with two apples, one in his mouth and the other in his hand. He handed it to Addie.

"Thank ya, child." Addie smiled.

"Ya be a good boy and mind what Addie says, ya hear. Thank ya, Addie."

"And ya stay safe," said Addie.

He turned and walked off. He could hear Addie sing for quite a distance.

Joshua fought the battle of Jericho
An' de walls came tumblin' down

Up to the walls of Jericho
He marched with spear in hand
"Go blow them ram horns," Joshua said
"Cause the battle is in my hands"

Then de lamb ram sheep began to blow
Trumpets began to sound
Joshua commanded the children to shout
An' de walls came tumblin' down

Joshua fought the battle of Jericho
An' de walls came tumblin' down

Malachi found the town of Shannon City in the same condition it was when he first saw it, desolate and in ruins. Walking down Main Street, he could hear the sound of hammers and saws in the distance. He could see the adults of his congregation working. Woody was clearly in charge. One of the landowners sat on horseback, overseeing every move. He held a rifle and wore a gun holster. They'd made two piles of rubble from the dilapidated old church. One pile, which was quite large, for building pieces that were in such disrepair they were no longer worth keeping. They'd burn these later. The other pile, which was smaller, consisted of building pieces worth saving – the church bell, doorknobs, a marble cross, and some other small items.

Malachi walked past the mounted overseer and up to the front of the church where Woody stood giving orders.

Woody spun around. "Pastor Jones, what are ya doin' here?"

"We need to talk, Woody."

"I know what you're gonna say, Pastor, but it ain't no good. It's this or else, and we've already had 'or else,' and it ain't pretty."

Percy came over to hear what was being said.

"Talk to this man," Malachi said to Percy, pointing at Woody. "This ain't right."

"I already have talked to him," Percy said. "And I know it ain't right, but I agree with him. We lived with these landowners all our lives. Ya don't understand what they're capable of doin'."

"No, I don't," Malachi said. "But I know ya never lived with them. Ya lived for them. And that's what you're gonna be doin' again if ya keep on this road. Ya got a chance here to walk away from slavery and never look back."

"And if we walk away, we get shot in the back," Woody added. "At least when we was slaves we ate regularly."

"Is that what motivates ya, your stomach?" Malachi asked.

"Partly, but it's our children's stomachs, too."

"And what about the children? You're sentencing them to a life as slaves," Malachi said, shaking his head. "This war is almost over. The South will lose. We are so close to ending slavery in this country. But it will never go away till two things happen."

Malachi waited till he was sure the next few words would be heard.

"Slavery will never die until Black Folk stand up against it, and White Folk stand up with them. Neither one can do it without the other. We've got a chance to do just that right here, this very day. On a small scale, yes; but if it don't start here and now, with ya and me, it'll never happen."

"Ya are willin' to go down the line with us? Stand with us to the bitter end, even if it means death?" asked Percy.

"As God as my witness, I will go the distance with ya."

Woody stood on the rotting staircase and shouted, "Listen everybody, stop what you're doin', and gather 'round. Pastor got somethin' to tell y'all."

The hammering and sawing stopped. They dropped pieces of wood to the ground and they gathered at the front of the old church. Woody stepped down to give the stairs to Malachi. The overseer took notice, moved his horse in closer, and put a firmer grip on his rifle.

Malachi stood at the top step and spoke as loud as he could.

"Friends, we stand today at the crossroads…you, me, the landowners, the North, the South. This entire country is at the crossroads. We can go in any direction we choose. We can go to the left, we can go right, or we can move forward. But I warn ya, we should never turn around and go back. Not back to the way we came. I can only image what the road y'all were on was like that got ya to this here crossroads. Do ya really wanna go back to the way it was? That's what will happen if ya let the landowners sway ya. Today you're fixin' the church, tomorrow it's a barn, then you're planting and pickin' crops, and then ya can move back onto the plantations, back a hundred years.

"We all need to stand up together and say 'No! We ain't gonna take it no more.' If not for yourselves, think of the children."

"But we are thinkin' of the chillun," shouted Alice Mobley. "Ya don't know how bad the owners can make life for ya and your chillun."

"All the more reason to stop it here and now," Malachi argued. "If ya care about the children, ya need to stop this now. Or it'll go on and on. If ya don't, the burden will be passed on to your children. Do ya want them to fight your fight? It has to happen someday, so then let it be today, and let it be with us."

"But how, how do we stop doin' what we've been doin' for so long?" someone asked.

"One day at a time, by stickin' together like a family, by puttin' your faith in God and your trust in one another. Ya do it through prayer and hard work. Become fearless."

Malachi bent down, picked up a stick of wood, and handed it to Woody. "Here, Woody. Ya know all about wood. What would it take to snap this here piece of wood?"

"Not much," Woody said as he snapped the stick in half.

Malachi bent down and picked up four sticks and handed them to Woody.

"How about now?" asked Malachi.

Woody tried with all his might, but he couldn't do it.

"Separately, ya could break every one of those sticks; but together they're too strong for ya. See what I'm sayin', folks? We can do it together. We just turn around, raise our heads high, put one foot in front of the other, and keep on walkin'."

Malachi stepped down and did an about-face only to be confronted with the mounted overseer pointing his rifle at him.

"Ya sure do talk a heap," said the overseer. "I don't think Jack would approve of ya riling these folks up." He poked his rife at Malachi. "Ya best be gettin' back to where ya came."

Malachi moved closer to the muzzle of the rifle. "What's your name?"

"Tom Bennett. Why?"

Malachi took hold of the rifle barrel, placing the muzzle on his chest, over his heart. "Well, Tom you're gonna have to shoot me 'cause I ain't gonna keep my mouth shut, and I ain't gonna leave unless these here folks come with me."

Tom, his mouth open, looked in confusion down at Malachi.

"Go ahead, shoot me!" Malachi insisted.

"I don't wanna shoot no reverend," said Tom.

"It's the only way," Malachi said. "Go ahead, shoot me!"

"And when you're done, ya can shoot me," Percy said.

"And then me," Woody added.

"And me," said one of the others.

"And me," they all said.

"And when you're done killin' us all, ya can go to their homes and kill their children, 'cause they won't have much longer to live with no one lookin' after them." Malachi pointed to the rubble behind him. "Ya see that, Tom. That used to be a church, a house of

God. Ya want these good people to rebuild it for ya, so ya got a place to worship. Is that the kind of god ya worship, Tom? Ya believe in a god who wants one man to own another man and kill him when he don't obey and then kill his children? Ya think God wants that for these people and their children. Why not ya and yours? What's the difference…skin color?"

"Ya talkin' crazy, preacher."

"Crazy? Or maybe you're scared `cause it's startin' to make sense to ya, and ya don't like it?"

Tom looked totally perplexed. "Jack and the others ain't gonna like this," he said, turning his horse around and riding off.

"That's one," said Malachi.

"Just another fifty million to go," replied Percy.

Malachi turned and started across town, the others marched alongside and behind him. They marched down Main Street, out of town, and down the old road till they got to the church.

"There is sure to be trouble," Malachi announced. "If there be any of ya who fears they can't go through with this, it's all right. We can hide ya and yours in the woods till this all blows over or we're all killed."

No one said a word or moved a muscle.

"Well then, y'all best be gettin' back to your homes and families; but before ya do, let us pray."

Malachi had learned that his congregation's favorite way of praying was in song.

I am free
I am free, oh Lord
I am free
I am washed by the blood of the lamb

You may knock me down
I will rise again
I am washed by the blood of the lamb
I fight you with my sword and shield
I am washed by the blood of the lamb

Remember the day, I remember it well
My dungeon shook and my chains fell off
Jesus came and made me clean
Said go in peace and sin no more
Glory to God; let your faith be strong
Lord, it won't be long before I'll be gone

I am free

A Slave's Song

I am free, oh Lord
I am free
I am washed by the blood of the lamb

Fourteen

Beams of Heaven

When everyone left, it was dark. Malachi started toward Addie's home to fetch Emmanuel. He found her on the porch, sitting in her rocking chair where he'd left her earlier that day.

"I didn't expect to find ya up," Malachi said.

"Don't ya know, old folks don't sleep much?" she said. "Wait till ya get to be my age, then you'll see. I like to sit out here at night and just watch the stars." She pointed off in the distance. "I like seein' the church steeple peekin' over the treetops. It does my heart good."

"Was Emmanuel a good boy?" Malachi asked.

"Oh, that child is always good. He fell asleep right after he ate supper. Ya know, ya could have left him for the night. I would have brought him in the mornin'."

"Nah, he likes waken up in his own bed. I'll just carry him home."

Malachi entered the shack, and came out a minute later with a limp sleeping Emmanuel in his arms.

"Thanks again, Addie. We'll see ya tomorrow."

"Ya be careful goin' home, Pastor."

It was only a half-moon, but enough light to make his way back to the church. It's not an uncommon thing to feel fear in the dark, and to feel someone is watching you. Malachi understood why he felt fear. After today, there would be much to fear. But he couldn't shake off the feeling of someone watching.

At the church, Malachi went in through the backdoor. He found his way into Emmanuel's bedroom. He placed him down on the bed, and smiled. He'd carried Emmanuel to bed many times, and every so often he would be aware the boy was growing and getting heavier. He took off Emmanuel's shoes and placed them under the bed. Quietly he left the room, closing the door behind him.

After heating up leftover morning coffee, Malachi sat at the kitchen table, looking out the backdoor. He reflected over the day's events. It was truly in God's hands; he had no idea what to do next. He went into his room, undressed and hung his clothes up, put on his nightshirt, and flopped down on his bed. He was asleep in minutes.

****

A metallic clicking sound woke Malachi. There was just enough moonlight seeping through his bedroom window to illuminate the figure of a man standing at his bedside, staring down at him. It was Tom Bennett. Before Malachi could say a word, Bennett pressed the muzzle of his handgun against Malachi's temple. That's when Malachi realized what the metallic sound that woke him was. It was the cocking of the gun now pressed to his head.

"Don't make a sound," said Bennett. "Jack's outside. He wants to have a few words with ya. Just get up slowly and walk out the back."

Bennett removed his gun from Malachi's head, but kept it aimed at him. He backed away as Malachi got out of bed. Bennett followed Malachi out of the bedroom and out of the house, his gun pressing into Malachi's ribs.

Outside, all the landowners stood by their horses. Jack Bates stood in front, shaking his head and smiling.

"Tom told me all about your big speech today, Reverend." Bates moved in close to Malachi. Without warning Bates brought his fist up into Malachi's stomach; he doubled over. "I tried to be nice about this, but it seems nice just don't work with your kind. Now I don't know what hold ya got on these colored folks, but ya better change your ways. Ya can't be scammin' them. They ain't got no money to scam. Or maybe you're in for the power. Well, either way, ya can keep doin' what your doin'; only from now on ya take your orders from me."

"I take my orders from God," Malachi said, slowly straitening up.

"Get off it, Reverend. Don't try to pull that holier-than-thou wool over my eyes. Save it for your darkie friends. No, what ya need is some educatin'. Once you're knocked down a peg or two, you'll be just fine."

Jack looked to his horse and gave a short soft whistle. The beast came over to his side.

"Ya see how nicely she obeys me? That's not because she loves me; it's because she fears me. I whipped this mare everyday till she feared me, and once she feared me, she obeyed me. And that's what I'm gonna do with ya. I'm gonna put the fear-a-god in ya. Only I'm gonna be your god." He backed away. "Hold him against the tree."

Two men took Malachi by the arms and brought him to the large hanging tree. They stood on either side of him and held his arms around the trunk of the tree. Jack removed his bullwhip from off his saddle. He wheeled it a few times, cracking the air.

"Ya see, Reverend, I'm a virtuoso with a bullwhip. I not only know how to wheel it, I know just how to use it on a man to get just the effect I desire. I can do it in such a way and so much that it kills ya. Understand that I have killed men with this very whip. All of them were slaves of mine. Or I can whip ya just in a way that will leave ya a cripple. Or I can leave ya in pain, where you'll need weeks, if not months, to recover. But don't worry, Reverend. I'm gonna give ya just enough to where you'll be hurtin' for a few days, but you'll be able to function. I just want ya to know the other options that I make available, in case ya don't come around to our way of thinkin'. Hold him tight!"

The two men pulled his arms with more force. Jack let the whip fly. It ripped through Malachi's nightshirt and through his skin. Malachi was taken aback by how much pain it caused. No wonder people died of whippings. How could anyone endure such punishment? The lash cut into Malachi's back once more, then again…six times in all.

"Let him go," Jack ordered.

The world spun around Malachi's head. He was unable to hold himself up. He fell to his knees, and then flat-face to the ground. Jack went to him, grabbed him by the hair, and raised his head, and spoke directly into Malachi's face.

"That was only six. Imagine a dozen, two dozen, or more. Tom told me about your speech on how folks bein' at the crossroads should never go back the way they came. Well, I agree. You're future is to be the pastor of the white church downtown. And to make sure ya go ahead with it, we're gonna burn the road ya came on. That way ya won't be tempted to go back the way ya came, especially when there ain't nothin' to go back to. Go ahead, boy, burn her down."

One of the men appeared holding a torch; another man lit it with a match. Another man kicked open the front door of the church. The first man hurled the lit torch into the church. The other man shut the door. Jack was still holding Malachi by the hair, making sure he had a good view of what was happening.

"Now ya got to come preach downtown, 'cause ya ain't got no other choice. Do yourself a favor and make it easy on yourself. If ya care anything about those darkies, make it easy on them, too. Don't fight it, Reverend; it's God's will."

Smoke started to seep out from under the front doors of the church, and billow from out the steeple above. Malachi saw the faint amber glow of flames through the windows of the church vestibule.

****

When Percy was a young man, he could sleep through anything. When he became a man and married and they had children, often he would have to get up in the middle of the night to see to or feed the babies. His ear became accustom to waking him with the slightest sound in the night. Being a father does that to some men, even heavy snorers like Percy. Years later, he never regained the ability to sleep through any out-of-the-ordinary sounds in the night. That's why the thuds of galloping horses going past his home nearly made him jump from the bed to the ceiling. He ran to the window to see the landowners with Jack Bates in the lead racing toward the church.

With a lit candle, he ran into his sons' bedroom. Just like their father was when he was young, they were in deep sleep, snoring. He had a difficult time waking them. Finally, he went to the kitchen and returned with a pitcher of water. He pulled back their covers and doused them both.

"Pa, what'd ya do that for?" Isaac said, chocking on the water.

"Jacob, Isaac, there's trouble at the church. Get dressed and meet me outside," Percy ordered.

The two jumped out of bed and pulled their nightshirts over their heads. Percy ran back in his room. He always kept the next day's clothes hung over a chair. He was in them in a flash. When he got outside, his sons were waiting for him.

"What is it, Pa?" Jacob asked.

"Don't know, but I just saw the landowners headin' for the church."

"Look there!" shouted Isaac, pointing east.

A thick billow of black smoke was rising in the sky over what was sure to be the church.

"Come on! We ain't got time to waste," Percy hollered, running off down the road, his sons, close behind.

After only a few yards, his young sons past him by; he did his best to keep up, his breath getting shorter with every few steps. Finally, he had to stop. He bent over, placed his hand on his knees, and tried to catch his breath. Once he was breathing somewhat normal, he took off again. He could see the backs of his sons up ahead.

Isaac was the first to get to the clearing where the church stood, followed close behind by his brother, Jacob. A moment later, Percy caught up with them. The three men stood motionless, staring in confusion and disbelief.

The front of the church was in flames, from the stairs up to the tip of the steeple. The flames were beginning to eat their way down both sides of the church. Lying face down before the church was their pastor, around him stood the landowners. They each took a turn at giving him a kick before they mounted their horses. Jack Bates was the last to kick Malachi and get atop his horse. He shouted something down at Malachi, but the roar of the flames was too loud for them to hear what was said. The band of horsemen took off down the road going east.

The three men came to their senses and ran for Malachi. Surprisingly, Percy was the first to reach him. He fell to his knees and lifted Malachi's head.

"Pastor, are ya all right?"

Suddenly, a sharp, shrill scream cut through the air. It came from the east, from down the road where the landowners galloped off on. It was a woman's voice.

Percy turned and looked up at his sons. "Jacob, go see what that was."

****

Addie had tried to sleep, but as she did most nights, she'd wake up in the middle of the night, dress and go sit in her rocking chair on the front porch. She'd like to read her Bible; but at her age, her eyes were no good for reading by candle light. She could only see things in dark shapes. So she'd sit outside till the sun came up, thinking, praying, and singing out loud.

> *I don't know how long it will be*
> *Nor for what the future holds for me*
> *But this I know, if Jesus leads me*
> *I shall have a home someday*

> *Often times my sky is clear*
> *Joy abounds without a tear*
> *Though a day so bright begun*
> *Clouds may hide tomorrow's sun*

Michael Edwin Q.

There'll be a day that's always bright
A day that never yields to night
And in its light the streets of glory
I shall behold some day

Harder yet may be the fight
Right may often yield to might
Wickedness awhile may reign
Satan's cause may seem to gain
There is a God who rules above
With hand of power and heart of love
If I am right, He'll fight my battle
I shall have peace someday

Burdens now may crush me down
Disappointments all around
Troubles speak in mournful sigh
Sorrow through a tear stained eye
There is a world where pleasure reigns
No mourning soul shall roam its plains
And to that land of peace and glory
I want to go someday

Beams of heaven, as I go
Through this wilderness below
Guide my feet in peaceful ways
Turn my midnights into days
When in the darkness I would grope
Faith always sees a star of hope
And soon from all life's grief and danger
I shall be free some day

Addie looked to the west, to the steeple of her beloved church. Flames licked the sides and tip of the pinnacle. She jumped to her feet, down the stairs, and down the road. She moved as fast as her old body would go. She prayed as she went. She prayed for the church. She prayed for Pastor Jones; and she prayed for little Emmanuel.

As she drew closer, she smelled smoke, the flickering orange glow of the flames shown through the trees and onto her face. Rounding the bend, she came on the church clearing. She saw her beloved church afire. She heard what she thought to be the sound of approaching thunder. Perhaps the Lord would send down a rain to quench the fire. But it wasn't thunder she heard. It was the sound of fast approaching horses. Too old to move out of the way quickly enough, the horsemen ran her down.

****

As Jacob ran off to investigate the scream, Percy and Isaac helped Malachi to his feet. Percy inspected Malachi's back.

"I've seen worse," Percy said. "You'll be hurtin' for a long while, but ya should be able to get around."

Malachi shook his head as if to clear his mind and think straight. "Emmanuel! Where is Emmanuel?" he shouted.

Malachi ran to the back of the church followed by Percy and Isaac. He rushed into the building through the backdoor. Smoke filled the kitchen, causing Malachi to hunker down to the floor to breath. He closed and covered his eyes as he made his way into Emmanuel's bedroom.

"Emmanuel! Emmanuel!" he shouted.

He ran his hands over the top of the bed – nothing. He reached under the bed and found no one. He did a quick surveillance of the room till he was sure Emmanuel wasn't there. When he could take it no more, he rushed out of the building, collapsing to the ground, choking from the smoke.

Percy and Isaac lifted him up.

"He wasn't there," Malachi exclaimed.

"Maybe, he got out and he's lookin' for ya?" Percy said.

They searched around the building. When they were midway on the left side of the building, they all heard something come from inside the church hall. It was the sound of someone franticly blowing into a mouth organ.

"Emmanuel!" Malachi cried.

Without a second thought he rushed into the burning building.

"Emmanuel!" he hollered over and over.

Everything was on fire, the walls, the floors, the pews, the overhead beams, the pulpit, even the organ. He followed the sound of the random notes blown on the mouth harp. He found Emmanuel hiding behind the organ, under the bellows. He gathered the child up in his arms and started for the front door. Just a few feet from the exit, one of the overhead beams, now a fiery block of wood, fell in front of them, blocking the way. Malachi looked around for another way out. He pushed one of the pews close to the wall. He hopped up on it and ran the length of pew. When he got to the end, he jumped. Covering as much of Emmanuel as he could, they went crashing through one of the windows.

He tumbled across the grass still holding the child close to him. When they stopped, Malachi let Emmanuel loose. Percy and Isaac took hold of Malachi and began rolling him on the ground. His nightshirt was on fire, but in no time they extinguished the flames. Emmanuel was crying. Malachi took him up in his arms to calm him.

"There, there, everything's gonna be all right," Malachi whispered in his ear.

Just then, Jacob came in view. He was holding Addie in his arms. There were tears in Jacob's eyes.

Malachi ran to them. He put his hand to her throat, and then his ear to her face.

"She's still alive," he announced. "Quick, let's take her home."

Fifteen

Carry Me Home

Jacob moved as quickly as he could, trying not to stumble in the dark, as he carried Addie to her home. His father, Percy, and his brother, Isaac, were at his side, but Malachi, holding Emmanuel's hand, lagged behind. Emmanuel was clearly upset and crying, not only from the ordeal he'd just suffered but to see his beloved Addie in such a state.

Addie's breathing was uneven and labored. You could hear the gurgle of liquid in her lungs. She was bleeding internally. Her eyes closed, she hovered between consciousness and unconsciousness. She moaned every time she shook in Jacob's arms. He tried to be careful for her sake, but there were too many rocks in the road.

At Addie's home, Jacob rushed in the house and placed her gently on her bed. Isaac went to the stove and stoked the fire. Percy fetched a towel, soaked it in a water bucket, and placed it on Addie's forehead. Malachi sat on the edge of the bed, holding her hand. Emmanuel sat on the floor in the corner, still crying.

"Addie, can ya hear me?" Malachi whispered.

"You're gonna be all right, Addie," Percy said.

"Percy, ya know as well as me it's a sin to lie," Addie said in a low voice. "An old woman ain't no match for a pack of horses."

"Ya just rest awhile," Malachi said.

"There'll be time enough for sleep before the sun rises," Addie said. She pointed to a shelf, a flat board nailed to the far wall. On it were three books. "Will ya get me my books, Percy?"

Percy took down the books, placing them on the bed at her side. It was a struggle but she took hold of the first book and pushed it toward Malachi.

"This here is my Bible. I want Emmanuel to have it." She looked into Malachi's eyes. "Ya gotta promise me you'll do everything ya can to make sure that boy is raised a good Christian. I don't wanna be in heaven for eternity, waiting for that sweet child to come and he never does. Ya gotta promise me."

"I promise," said Malachi.

She pushed the next book toward Percy who stood at the foot of her bed.

"That there is my hymnal. It's got all the good church songs in it. Many a night, I sat alone in this here room singin' praises. It always took away the pain and loneliness"

She pushed the last of the three books to Malachi.

"I know ya don't need it. You're a good preacher, Pastor Jones. But I think you'll like it. It's always helped me."

Malachi opened to the first page and read the cover. "The Imitation of Christ and the Contempt for the Vanities of the World" by Thomas A. Kempis (1379-1471), She placed her hand on the book and quoted from it.

My son, to the degree that you can leave yourself behind
To that degree will you be able to enter into me

"Don't ask me how I got that book. It weren't by Christian means. But that's all past now. As a young girl, as a young slave girl, I didn't know what little freedom I truly had. I only knew the world I lived in: Massa and slaves. When I grew up, I realized how much of the world, how much of life was denied me. I became angry and bitter. It was like a stone in my heart that I carried in me for years. Oh, I heard the word of the Lord many times, but it was just words without any meaning. I read the Bible over and over, looking for some hope, but it was just words. Till one day the Spirit came upon me, and it all made sense. The Lord took me by the hand and opened my fist and placed his hand in mine. Then he took that stone out of my heart, and he crawled inside, and He's been livin' in that space since then."

She was sounding weaker. Her eyes were just half-open slits.

"Percy, do me one last good turn. Take the pain from me. Open the hymnal to page ninety-six. That's my favorite. Sing me home, brother, sing me home."

Percy's hands were shaking, but he found the page. His voice cracked over and over, but he somehow got through it.

I am tired and weary but I must toil on
Till the Lord come to call me away
Where the morning is bright and the lamb is the light
And the night is as fair as the day

There the flowers will be blossoming, the grass will be green
And the skies will be clear and serene
The sun ever shines, giving one endless beam
And the clouds there will ever be seen

There the bear will be gentle, the wolf will be tame
And the lion will lay down with the lamb
The host from the wild will be led by a Child
I'll be changed from the creature I am

No headaches or heartaches or misunderstands
No confusion or trouble will be
No frowns to defile, just a big endless smile
There'll be peace and contentment for me

There'll be peace in the valley for me some day
There'll be peace in the valley for me
I pray no more sorrow and sadness or trouble will be
There'll be peace in the valley for me

As the last note was sung, a silence fell over the world. Addie was gone. Percy closed the hymnal and pressed it to his breast. Malachi held his book and ran his hand over the cover. Emmanuel stood up and walked to the bedside and fell down upon Addie. The boy cried into her neck. Malachi placed his hand on Emmanuel's back and lovingly ran his hand from shoulder to shoulder.

"It all right, Emmanuel, it's all right. It's gonna be all right."

The morning sunlight poured into the small room and flooded it golden.

****

Everyone decided that Malachi and Emmanuel would live in Addie's house till they finished building the new church on the same site as the old. Some of the couples in the congregation brought clothing that their children had outgrown for Emmanuel. As for Malachi, some of the men donated pants, shirts, and shoes, mostly work-clothes. But best of all, he received a new black suit from Abner Taylor.

Abner told the story of the suit to Malachi. "It was my brother Joseph's suit. He used to wears suits when he worked. He was a house slave on Jack Bates' plantation. He died the week he received this new suit; he never got a chance to wear it. We were gonna bury him in it; but everyone thought it was a waste to put a new suit in the ground. So, we buried him in one of his old suits. The family decided, since I was his brother and we were the same size, that I should get the suit. But to tell ya the truth, Pastor, walkin' around in your dead brother's suit is mighty uncomfortable, even if it is a perfect fit. So, if ya don't have any qualms about wearin' a dead man's suit…he never even got to wear it…than you're welcome to it."

"How'd your brother die?" Malachi asked.

"Jack Bates hung him, hung him from that big tree on the church property. Over the years, I'd say the owners must have hung at least twenty slaves from that tree."

"And Pastor Davis, so I've been told," Malachi added.

"Yeah, and him too," Abner agreed. "One day somebody ought to chop that thing down and use if for firewood."

"Why did Bates hang your brother?" Malachi asked.

"I told ya Joseph was a house slave. Well, one night his job was to serve dinner to the Bates family. The first course was soup, hot soup. Joseph had the misfortune of spillin' an entire bowl into Jack Bates' lap. They hung him that very night."

"Ya mean to tell me Jack Bates killed your brother because he accidently dropped hot soup on him?"

115

Abner laughed. "No offense, Pastor, but I can tell ya don't know much about slavery. A slave is nothin' more than another man's property, not different from a horse or chicken. I've seen slaves killed for less. I've seen men killed because they got sick and couldn't do their job fast enough or they knocked somethin' over and broke it. I've seen men killed because their hand accidentally brushed up on a white woman. Worst of all, I seen men killed just for the enjoyment of killin'."

This statement caught Malachi off-guard, leaving him speechless for a moment.

"I'm sorry to hear that, Abner. But I thank ya for the suit."

"Don't mention it. My wife took some black material and a piece of white material off that shirt's cuff to make a proper preacher's collar. Ya look just like the preacher from that picture inside the hymnals."

"That was very kind of her," Malachi commented. "I'll thank her for it later."

Later meant after Addie' funeral. The congregation assembled at the clearing at the bottom of the hill where the church once stood. Over the years, many a beloved passed-on member had been buried there, including Pastor Davis. They stood around the gapping mouth of the grave. Woody did a fine job with the coffin. He even made a small cross and burned Addie's name into it.

Malachi stood before the congregation. "Friends, we are here today to show our love and give a farewell to our beloved sister, Addie. She was the backbone of this church, not only in her musical ability but also in how much she gave of herself. I have no doubts she is in heaven this day. I know when she stands before the Lord she will hear, 'Well done, good and faithful servant!' Before we go on, is there anything anyone would like to share?"

Percy raised his hand. "When my wife died, I was lost with two boys to raise. Addie helped me get started. She taught me how to put my house in order. She was like a mother to us all."

"When I was sick one winter, she brought me food everyday, even on days it snowed," said Molly Stewart.

"She helped me birth both my babies. Stayed up all night and helped me deliver," added Betsy Brown.

On and on people testified to the great soul they had loved and would miss.

Eli Johnson stepped forward. "I loved Addie, just like all the rest of ya; and I'll miss her, too, just like all the rest of ya. But I'll be doggone if I just stand here and help y'all put her in the ground and just go home and forget it.

"I say we take revenge. They kill one of ours, we kill one of theirs. An eye for an eye, I say. If we don't do anything, they're just gonna keep on bein' what they is, a pack of wolves. I say we go get 'em."

"But they got guns," one of the young men said.

Eli pointed off into the distance. "There are dead soldiers all over these hills, each with a rifle or a pistol or both. If we go lookin', we can have all the guns and ammunition we need."

"You're just talkin' crazy," said one of the older men.

"I'll tell ya what's crazy," Eli said, "sittin' around for them to get strong again, so we can all wind up back on the plantations and under their thumbs. I say we get 'em while they're down, when they're weak. Don't wait for them to get back on their feet, kick 'em when down, because if they ever get up again, we'll never get up at all. Who's with me?"

Some of the younger men raised their hands. Eli turned and started off into the woods. Three of the other men followed.

"Eli, don't do it," cried Bessie, Eli's wife. She broke down in tears and rested her head on an other woman's shoulder.

"Eli, stop! Don't go. We can talk this out," Malachi shouted.

He felt a hand on his shoulder; he turned to see Percy.

"Don't waste your breath, Pastor. I've raised two young boys; and I've seen it all before. He's just young, and he's hurt. Give him some time to lick his wounds. He'll be back."

"I hope so," Malachi said.

"Let's just get this poor woman in the ground," Percy whispered.

Malachi continued the ceremony.

"Friends, brothers and sister, in sure and certain hope of the resurrection to eternal life through our Lord Jesus Christ, we commend to Almighty God our sister Addie, and we commit her body to the ground. Earth to earth; ashes to ashes; dust to dust. The Lord bless her and keep her, the Lord make his face to shine upon her and be gracious onto her and give her peace. Amen."

"Amen."

They slowly and gently lowered the coffin into the grave. Everyone threw wild flowers down onto the coffin. As they shoveled the dirt down, the cold thump of earth hitting the wood coffin brought home the reality of what was truly happening. They broke down and cried; yet still, with tears in their eyes, they sang.

Swing low, sweet chariot
Comin' for to carry me home

I looked over Jordon, and what did I see
Comin' for to carry me home
A band of angels comin' after me
Comin' for to carry me home

If you get there before I do
Comin' for to carry me home
Tell all my friends I'm comin' too
Comin' for to carry me home

I'm sometimes up, I'm sometime down
Comin' for to carry me home

Michael Edwin Q.

But still my soul feels heaven bound
Comin' for to carry me home

Swing low, sweet chariot
Comin' for to carry me home

Sixteen

Hard Trails

It was comfortable living in Addie's home; but it seemed strange; her presence could be felt throughout the room. All the articles were her belongings. Her few bits of clothing hung from a hook by the door. But what was most prevalent was her scent that permeated everything, especially the bed which Malachi allowed Emmanuel to sleep in. He was happy to bring the rocking chair in from off the porch each night and sleep in that.

Emmanuel's speech was developing very slowly. His daily vocabulary consisted of five words...yes, no, hello, goodbye, and Papa. It was still far better than the silence he'd come from; so Malachi kept his disappointment to himself and waited patiently, encouraging and gently coaxing the boy whenever possible.

The work on the new church was slow. Folks had their hands full just keeping alive. But each of them donated as much time as possible.

First, they needed to haul the remains of the old church away and clear the area. New wood was needed. Of course, Woody was in charge of seeking out the finest trees. All of which were not close by. They would fell the tree and saw off the branches, and then drag it back to the church site. There they would slowly saw as many planks from the tree as possible. It would be some time before the true work of building the structure would commence.

Except for Sundays, the mundane of everyday life filled their days, such as gathering wood and food, cooking, cleaning, and washing clothes. True to his word, Malachi read a Bible passage every night to Emmanuel and then tried giving an explanation of the passage to Emmanuel in a way he could understand. At that point, boredom would weight heavily on the boy. His eye lids would flutter, then close, and finally sleep.

Late at night as Emmanuel slept, Malachi often worked on the Sunday sermon. It had become increasingly difficult since Pastor Davis' notes and letters were destroyed in the fire, as well as the Bible Marcellus gave to him. Having an extra Bible, the Brown family, to Malachi's delight and deep appreciation, gave him one as a gift. He studied the Bible intensely, often referring to passages he found in the book Addie bequeathed him.

It was on one particular night that Malachi, lost for ideas for a sermon, decided to snoop through Addie's belongings. He had hesitated to rummage through her stuff, feeling he was showing disrespect, which was nonsense, as it would have to be done sooner or later.

Looking in every nook and cranny, Malachi found very little of anything of value, other than a few bricks of homemade lye soap, a cameo brooch of a woman holding a flower, and a small sewing box. In the box were a few spools of different color threads, a collection of various size sewing needles, and a large pair of scissors. There was nothing of interest under the bed, save for an ancient chamber pot, so it seemed at first glance.

After closer inspection, he saw an envelope pressed between the bed slats and the mattress. Trying not to wake Emmanuel, he carefully and gently retrieved the envelope Luckily, Emmanuel was a heavy sleeper.

The envelope must have been white at one point in time, perhaps years ago; but now it was faded yellow. It was packed with papers for it was thick in his hands. On the front of the envelope was written:

"To be opened after my death"

If it was Addie's handwriting, it surprised Malachi. The script was flowery, and clearly made by someone educated. Not what you'd expect from someone who'd been a slave all her life.

He opened the unsealed envelope and took out a handful of papers. They too must have been white, now yellowed with age. The writing was the same fine hand as that on the outside of the envelope. He moved the rocking chair close to the table, sat down, moved the lit candle closer, laid the papers out flat, and began to read.

If you are reading this, I am surely dead. I do hope it is being read by friendly eyes. I hope it is someone who will not think or speak too harshly of me; someone who can find something good in my story and pass it on. It is as much a confession as it is testament to faith and hopefully an encouragement to those who come after me.

I am second generation born a slave in this country. When I was young and heard the older folks talk of Africa, it was like they were speaking about some mythical realm I could not imagine. They told me their true tribal names and what they meant. I felt cheated. I had no homeland and no tribal name. My true identity was stolen from me long before I was born.

My parents were young when they married and had me, in their teens. They were the property of Ahriman Wolff, slave and plantation owner.

It was a large and fine property, the Wolff Plantation. My parents worked the land for him and picked his cotton, like so many other slaves. We lived in a communal shack with few amenities and no privacy. When I was old enough to get around on my own and grasp items well enough, I was sent to the fields as a picker with the others.

It was a long, hard day of work, and it was a seven-day work week. Being raised in this manner, I had no idea life could be any different. As a young girl, I believed white folks to be superior to black folks, and that they deserved their place in life and all the property, including slaves, went with it. I believed blacks to be inferior.

A Slave's Song

Destined to be slaves, and justified to be subservient. My entire world confirmed this to be true, and no one, including my own parents, told me otherwise.

It's not that my parents didn't love, care, or guide me. It was just that they too did not know better; and if they were to teach me anything, it would be to survive. The first years of my life, I received little instruction in anything else. It was forbidden to teach a slave to read or write. Without books, one must travel to receive knowledge. We were imprisoned on the plantation. We knew little of the outside world.

As for spiritual guidance, I was told there was a God. I would say my prayers at night. Prayers consisting of asking for blessings for everyone in my world, my father and mother, the other slaves, the other children, and lastly, a blessing over the master of the house and his family.

When I turned eleven, my entire world changed. Not all at once, but major changes in quick succession. The first drastic change was when my father died; actually he was killed, hung for whatever reason I never learned. Ahriman Wolff ordered the hanging of my father. The overseers marched us to the largest tree on the plantation. We were all forced to watch his execution, as a warning and a lesson. With his hands tied behind his back, mounted on a horse, and a noose around his neck tied to the tree. My father said his goodbyes to his wife and friends. For me, all he offered was a tearful glance, which I reciprocated in kind. With one swift slap to the horse, it ran off, leaving my father dangling from the noose. When there is no long drop where your neck is broken, hanging is a slow and painful way to die. My father's eyes bugged out of his head, his tongue wagged in his mouth, and his legs kicked wildly. An overseer doused him with kerosene and set him on fire. A minute later my father went motionless. The lower half of his body was scorched. They left him hanging there for three days. Each day there was less of him, as birds feasted on him. At first, I was heartbroken. The sadness was overpowered by the horror, which turned to anger and a strong need for revenge. But in time, once I realized retribution would never be, I became engulfed in hopelessness and resolved to a life of despair.

The ordeal left my mother devastated. She went deep within herself never to emerge again. She seldom spoke. She ate little, till she was a skeleton with dead eyes staring off into nothingness. She never gave the overseers a full day's work. In return she was punished with whipping after whipping, which she suffered without ever crying out. In time, she withered away; and one night she died in her sleep. I was left to fend for myself. But even at the tender age of eleven, I had the strength and the knowledge on how to survive.

A few years after the death of my mother, the most unexpected thing happened. Another young slave girl, Tess, two years my senior, and I were summoned to the main house. There we were told we were to be schooled along with the Wolff children, their sixteen-year-old daughter Azazel, and their fourteen-year-old son Ubel.

Being young and naïve, I was clueless as to what was the reasoning for it all. The older and wiser Tess sat me down and explained what was to happen. She and I were chosen to be breeders. To increase the Wolff dynasty by giving birth to as many male slaves as possible. It was believed that if we were to be educated and pampered, the offspring would be of a higher quality. Of course, the fathers would be chosen from the smartest, strongest, and hardest working males to be found in the county.

I was too young, of course, but I was approaching the age of childbearing quickly. Tess, on the other hand, was at the age. Neither one of us was given a say; we were told what our futures would be. We were each given a small cabin to live in, which in time we would share with our respective and future male counterparts. We no longer had to work on the plantation. We were kept clean and well-dressed. They fed us well, to keep us healthy. All in all, our lives were far superior to the other slaves on the plantation.

As for our education, a tutor came each day to the main house to school the Wolff children. Normally, we would not be taught along with them. But to save on cost, we were schooled along with Azazel and Ubel. The tutor's name was Cyril Runt. He was a tall, slender man with a large hawk-like nose, which he used for looking down on the world. He had a fierce temper, taking it out on the Wolff children verbally, and Tess and me physically, though never so brutally as to scare us or ruin our health.

Azazel was a beautiful young woman with blue eyes, blonde hair, fair skin, a willowy body, and the face of an angel, but looks can be deceiving. For someone so young, she manifested many evils. She was vain, selfish, angry, cruel, and conniving. It was clear from the beginning she hated Tess and me.

Her younger brother, Ubel, was a male image of his sister with the same angelic good looks. Only the boy possessed a heart of gold. He was warm, friendly, and giving; everything his sister wasn't. Often Azazel would rebuke him for his kind ways, but it never deterred him from doing what came naturally to him, which came from his splendid heart.

Because of our special treatment, the other slaves treated us as outsiders. In time, the only friend I had in the world was Tess, not including some stolen moments of friendship and kindness from Ubel, when his sister wasn't looking. Tess and I became a family of two. That is until the master had one of the young male slaves move in with Tess. He was to remain living with her until she became pregnant. Failure to do so would be detrimental to both of them. I saw little of Tess during that time. Finally, she was with child. The male slave was moved out of Tess' shack and back into the slave community. Tess was treated like royalty during her pregnancy, and more so after she gave birth to a baby boy. After all, she was increasing her master's wealth.

For months, Tess was beside herself with joy. She never let the child from her sight. For the first time in her life she was truly happy. That is until tragedy struck. Once the child was weaned, Ahriman Wolff decided it best not to wait for the child to grow up before he could profit from his investment. He ordered the baby taken from Tess and sold to a traveling slave trader. Not able to bear the sorrow of losing her child, Tess killed herself; she cut her wrists. We learned about Tess during one of Mr. Runt's classes. Azazel Wolff broke into laughter at the news. I became so enraged, I slapped her. Mr. Runt bent me over a chair and with a switch whipped the tops of my thighs, high enough for Master Wolff to never see the scares, which I still have to this day. Azazel Wolff was no longer just an evil child, she'd become my sworn enemy.

The day came when I was to mate with one of the male slaves. In many ways, I was still a child, but physically able to become pregnant. His name was Clayton, in his late teens, though in many ways still a boy. He was strong and handsome, very muscular, which was probably why they chose him. He moved in to my little shack with me. It was very awkward. We weren't to be married, which at the time didn't mean much to me. I had no sights on any man, or having a child, but I had no say in the matter.

Clayton was a kind and understanding young man. I never fell in love with him, but in time I did feel comfortable with him. We eventually became close and intimate. Not that feelings played a part in it. If we didn't perform, we'd be in a world of trouble and pain. Months went by with no success. Ahriman Wolff gave us a warning. We had four months, or else. Luckily, that's what happened. Once I was with child, Clayton was removed from my life. Though we never married or fell in love, I would miss him.

During the next nine months, I was treated like royalty. The night I had the baby, the Wolff family doctor saw me through it, not the midwife. Thankfully, it was a male child. This pleased Ahriman Wolff and kept me in his good graces.

What I write now, I'm sure you will find shocking. I never named the child, and purposely refused to make any emotional ties. It was that or go mad and end up like Tess. As in the case with Tess, once the child was weaned, the child was sold.

And so the years went on. I went from one male partner to the next. I had a child every two years. They were breeding us like animals. I never named any of them, for all were taken from me after they were weaned. Sadly, the girl babies, thankfully there were only a few, were taken from me before being weaned. Knowing the master considered female infants a disappointment and a wasted investment, I can only image what happened to those poor babies.

The years passed on the plantation. My life was a lonely one. I was shunned by my own kind. Thankfully, Azazel Wolff, who antagonized me whenever and however possible, grew into beautiful woman with many suitors. She soon married and left our lives. Ubel, too, had grown. He was a dashing and handsome young man. I would say he was my only friend. He'd visit me now and then, bringing me books and treats from the house. That is, whenever he could do so without his sister finding out. When she left the plantation, his visits were more often.

It was on one particular cold winter night that there was a knock at my door. It was Ubel with a gift of a bottle of wine. He said it would warm me, and it did. We shared the drink. I'd never had wine or any form of alcohol in my life. It didn't take much to get me giddy. Oh, how we laughed. In my confused state, I didn't realize what was happening. I found myself on my bed with Ubel on top of me. I begged him to stop, but he was too lost in passion. I cried and pleaded to no avail. I felt it wrong. The others were loveless relations, but they were forced upon me. This was different. I tried to fight him off. He was too strong for me. I reached to my nightstand. Reaching for my sewing kit, I took a hard grasp of my scissors and plunged it into his back. He went stiff for a moment and then fell limp upon me. He was dead.

Understandably fearing the worst, I dragged his limp body out of my shack and into the cotton field, and left him there. When they found him the next day, his father went into a rage. The slaves were questioned. Many of them tortured for an answer. Some of them died. I felt guilty. I never could have foreseen what my actions would cause.

A Slave's Song

When I turned thirty, it became apparent I was no longer able to bear children. Ahriman Wolff and his wife had grown old and passed on. His daughter, Azazel, returned to take possession of the family plantation and all its slaves. I feared for my life. But to my surprise, I was sold. My new master was Jack Bates.

I became a house slave. As difficult as it was, my lot was still better than most other slaves. In my new surroundings with people who knew nothing of my past, I made friends, and for the first time in my life was relatively happy. But I was still empty inside.

It was when Pastor Davis came to Shannon City that again my life changed, and this time for the better. To the pastor and everyone else's surprise, when Pastor Davis tried to start a church in the area, instead of meeting opposition he was met with open arms by the landowners, led by my master, Jack Bates. Master had the inclination and convinced the other landowners that religion was a way of soothing the unhappy and rebellious nature of the slaves. They donated materials and allowed many of the slaves time off from their daily workload to erect the church structure. In just a few months, the building was up, and Sunday services were held every week.

In the beginning, attendance was low. At first, it was mostly women who made up the congregation, yours truly excluded. Most of the men refused to go, not wanting to give up what they considered the little pleasures in life that helped a slave get through life, namely drinking and carousing.

As for me, I saw no need for what I thought religion to be – a crutch. Little did I know how crippled I was inside and in need of a crutch.

One Sunday, I woke early. The sun shone through my window like gold. The sky was a deep blue. Clearly, the world was beautiful; but I didn't see or feel it, I only felt an emptiness that nothing seemed to fill. As if by instinct or impulse, I got out of bed, got dressed and headed in the direction of the church. As I walked, a strange feeling came over me, as if it weren't me doing the walking, as if it weren't of my own free will. As I approached the church, I could hear them singing.

> *Oh, the foxes have holes in the ground*
> *And the birds have their nests in the air*
> *And everything has a hidin' place*
> *But us poor sinners ain't got nowhere*

> *Now ain't them hard trails*

Michael Edwin Q.

Great tribulation
Hard trails, hard trails
I'm bound to leave this land

You may go this way
You may go that way
You may go from door to door
But if you haven't the good Lord in your heart
The Devil will get you sure

Now ain't them hard trails
Great tribulations
Hard trail, hard trails
I'm bound to leave this land

I entered the church and walked slowly up the aisle. The singing stopped, and all heads turned, and every eye was upon me. Pastor Davis came down from the pulpit and put his hand on my shoulder and smiled without saying a word. I turned to the congregation and said not a word. I began to cry.

There is something in every human being that knows the language of tears, for all have shed them. I didn't have to say a word, and they knew what was in my heart. Instead of laughing or criticizing, they all came to the front of the church to greet me. One by one, they hugged me and told me it was going to be all right, and I believed them. Which made me cry the more; and some of them began to cry and join in with me. I looked up and renounced my sins, and accepted the Lord. And in that moment, that emptiness within me was filled. I was on the road to glory; and I was never going to look back.

Blessing on you all,
Addie

Malachi sat for a moment, staring at the letter. Then slowly and gently he folded it, returning it to the envelope. Still holding the envelope, he stood up, and as softly as he could to not wake Emmanuel, he walked over to the bedside to check on the boy.

Emmanuel was sleeping fast. His long eyelashes fluttered as he dreamed. He looked like an angel. Malachi took hold of the blanket's edge, bringing it up to Emmanuel's chin. Not able to resist the urge, he placed his hand on the boy's head, gently soothed his brow, and then he bent low and kissed the boy on his forehead.

Trying not to stumble or kick anything as he moved around the room, he made it toward the makeshift shelf on the far wall where the sewing kit was and the two books Addie left Emmanuel and him. He took down the Bible she'd left to Emmanuel, opened it, and behind the front cover, he placed the letter. He closed the book, returning it to its place on the shelf.

He returned to the table, bent down, and blew out the candle. The room went dark, darker still since he'd been staring into the flame. Slowly, his eyes adjusted to the darkness; and he could make out various shapes of things.

He took hold of the rocking chair and went out with it onto the front porch. He sat down and began to rock himself to sleep. The night air was cool. He looked up to the heavens. It was a good night to sleep out under the stars.

Seventeen

When I Get to Heaven

Sometimes you can tell it's Sunday. There's a feel to it like no other day in the week. This particular Sunday was one of those. The air was crisp and clean; the sunlight was bright but not harsh or too hot, just warm and comfortable. The scent of nature, the flowers, trees, and grass, lingered about. The soft, gentle sound of the wind played a harmonic song, accompanied by the sound of crickets.

Malachi let Emmanuel sleep while he cooked breakfast. The boy must have been hungry because the smell of coffee and buttery wheat cakes woke him. He stood in the kitchen doorway rubbing the sleep from his eyes.

"Breakfast?" Emmanuel asked – another new word he'd added to his vocabulary.

"Just a few more minutes," Malachi said. "Ya got just enough time to wash up."

Emmanuel returned to his room. Malachi could hear him sloshing in his water basin.

"Don't forget…behind the ears," Malachi shouted.

After saying Grace, they ate in silence, Malachi with a pencil and paper making some last-minute changes to his sermon for that day.

Standing on the porch, they both took one last look at each other. Malachi straightened Emmanuel's collar. Malachi posed for Emmanuel.

"How do I look?" he asked the boy.

Emmanuel crooked his finger a few times to signal for Malachi to lean down. He licked his hand to wet it, and then ran it down the back of Malachi's head to flatten down his cowlick – it worked.

"Thank you," Malachi said, feeling a bit unnerved.

Emmanuel smiled and nodded.

They walked hand-in-hand up the road toward the church clearing. There were a few folks there already with others showing up in succession. Where the old church had stood was now an open area covered with grass. They'd decided to use it for Sunday service till a new building could be put up. Some folks brought chairs; others put down blankets and sat on the ground.

Malachi stood where the pulpit used to be, and the congregation sat where the pews used to be. There was no reason to do things that way, but old habits die hard. Besides, that was the way the new church building would be laid out. They could see it in their minds.

When Malachi was sure most folks were there, he opened in prayer.

"Blessings on y'all. Lord, we come here today to sing and praise ya, to live, and to learn, and love ya and to love one another. We thank ya for this day and our brothers and sisters. And all God's children said…?"

"Amen!"

A Slave's Song

It would be difficult singing a hymn without Addie's organ playing. It was times like this which brought her to everyone's mind and when folks missed her most. Still, they sang. Malachi started them off, and everyone joined in.

I got shoes, you got shoes
All God's children got shoes
When I get to heaven goin' to put on my shoes
Goin' to walk all over heaven all day

I got a harp, you got a harp
All God's children got a harp
When I get to heaven goin' to play on my harp
Goin' to play all over heaven all day

I got a crown, you got a crown
All God's children got a crown
When I get to heaven goin' to put on my crown
Goin' to shout all over heaven all day

I got a song, you got a song
All God's children got a song
When I get to heaven goin' to sing a new song
Goin' to sing all over heaven all day

Malachi waited for the hush to settle on the congregation. There was a cool breeze that felt good. He felt pleased to see Eli Johnson and his wife, Bessie, standing in the front. He wondered if Eli still held a hunger for revenge over the death of Addie. He made a mental note to speak with the young man after service. He looked from face to face and smiled.

"It's good to see y'all here today. I'm so proud of each and every one of ya. Some folks might say it ain't no use to go to church because there ain't one. But we know better. There is one. It's right here, and I can see it in your faces. Because a church ain't a building; it ain't four walls, a floor, and a ceiling. It's the Lord's children gathered together to praise him, hear the word, and go out into the world and spread the Good Word in love. And that's why I say we are here in church today."

Everyone smiled back at Malachi.

"One day we will have a church building, bigger and better than what stood here before; and we'll have stained glass windows and an organ..." Malachi stopped when he realized what he'd done. When he spoke of a church organ, it was clear it reminded everyone of Addie. He bowed his head. "Yeah, I miss her, too. But that's all the more reason we need to press on. And we can do it, because we're friends and neighbors and brothers and sisters, and because we are a church."

The entire congregation let out a loud, "Amen."

"And because we are…"

Malachi was stopped midsentence by the sound of horses galloping into the clearing. Everyone turned to see who it was – it was the landowners with Jack Bates in the lead. They nearly ran over the people standing in the back row. They dismounted, and stood looking at the congregation. One by one they took their guns out of their holsters, and the ones holding rifles held them up, pointing them into the crowd. Jack Bates with his pistol in his hand walked to the front, up to Malachi, brought his gun up and pointed it at Malachi's head. They all gasped. Holding the gun to Malachi's head, he turned and addressed his audience.

"Ya see where this has got ya? This is what I get for being nice. Like they say, 'Too good, no good'." He shouted at Malachi. "We could have worked together. Every body would have got what they wanted. Well now you're a dead man. Once you're gone, my troubles are over." He shouted to everyone. "Ya heard of the Fear of God. Well, let me tell ya. From here on in, I'm god around here; and y'all gonna fear me. Oh, I ain't gonna shoot him. I want something that's gonna stick in your memories. Something that will let ya know I mean business; and that I'm someone to fear. Because, once your pastor's dead, things are gonna start gettin' back to the way they was."

Malachi searched the faces of the congregation. They were all in shock with their eyes wide and their mouths open. That is except one. Malachi looked directly at Eli Johnson, whose eyes were aflame with anger and his fists tight with hatred. Malachi shook his head to dissuade Eli, but it was clear he was too far gone. But it wasn't only Eli who read what was in Malachi's eyes. As soon as Eli began to lunge forward, both of Percy's sons grabbed him and wrestled him to the ground.

"That's good, that's good. No need to get anyone else killed over one hot-head," Jack said.

When they felt sure Eli calmed down enough not to do anything rash, they let him up.

His wife, Bessie, clung to his side, holding his arm, and whispered to him, "Please, dear, don't. I understand how you feel, but you mustn't."

Eli clinched his fist and ground his teeth watching the scene play out before him, unable to do anything. The others felt the same.

"Now, where were we? Ah, yes, I was just about to blow your pastor's brains out. But like I said, I want to make a lasting impression on y'all; so we're goin' to do somethin' special. I know you've seen it many times before, but it never fails to get the point across." Jack looked to his men. "All right, boys, get the rope ready."

The men moved into position near the hanging tree, the one on the church property. The one they used so many times over so many years to make an example of so many rebellious slaves, men and women, and one uncooperative preacher – Pastor Davis. And now it was to be Malachi's turn.

It was a large rope, long and thick, like the kind you see used on small riverboats. One end was a hangman's noose. They threw that over the largest branch on the tree. It dangled ten feet off the ground. The other end they tied around the trunk of the tree.

Still holding the gun on Malachi, Jack maneuvered him past the crowd and toward the tree.

"Somebody, help him!" cried one of the women.

"That's right," Jack laughed. "Who wants to die with their pastor? We've got enough rope; and we've certainly got enough bullets."

No one said another word. They stood watching with cold stares as Jack pushed Malachi to the tree. They brought a horse to stand under the hangman's noose.

Jack started to laugh out loud. The other landowners smiled, wondering what he was thinking.

"What's so funny, Jack?"

"I just thought of somethin'. How many hangings have we done on this tree?"

"I don't know; maybe a dozen or more. Why?"

"In all those hangings, have we ever hung a white man?"

The men took time to think.

"There was Felipe."

"He don't count. Mexicans are lighter than most slaves; but they still ain't white."

Jack turned towards Malachi so the two could face each other.

"Well, Pastor, it seems you're the first. But then again, I wonder how white ya really are. I mean, what did ya expect? Ya eat with 'em, ya live with 'em. As far as I'm concerned, we still ain't hung a white man." He looked to the others. "Get him ready."

One of the men took hold of Malachi; and with leather straps tied his hands together behind his back. Then they guided him to the side of the horse. With tied hands, Malachi was unable to be of assistance in mounting the horse. It took three strong men a full minute to get him in the saddle. One of the men on horseback reached over and put the noose around Malachi's head. Then he pulled the rope tight till the knot dug into Malachi's neck and he began to choke and cough, barely able to breath.

"Do ya have any last words for your congregations, Pastor Jones?" Jack announced.

Seated up high, Malachi was able to see every face clearly. His mind was racing, leaving him unable to focus long enough on one thought long enough to speak. First, fear swept over him. Then he prayed for a miracle. His fear led to confusion, which led to a hopelessness he'd never known. To know you will be dead in the next moment is all consuming. Yet, something within him drove all those thoughts of misgivings aside; and the concern for others consumed him. He looked down into Jack's smiling face.

"I don't know if y'all understand what I'm about to say, but I'm going to try anyways." Malachi took a long pause before continuing. "I forgive ya; I forgive y'all."

The smile left Jack Bates' face and a look of shear hatred took its place.

Malachi looked out on his congregation.

"My friends, my brothers and sisters, I know ya will understand what I'm about to say." Again, he paused. "Do not revenge me. I know you're first gut reaction will be to do so, to strike back. Ya must let go of that anger, as ya must learn to let me go. But listen well. Do not...ever...give in to these men. They seek to enslave ya once more; and if ya return to the

131

old ways, ya will never be free again. It will be hard at first. There will be much suffering and hardship. But wasn't there suffering and hardship before? Life will always have these; and ya can meet them as slaves or as free people. Just remember y'all are children of God and that He loves ya no more or less than anyone else. I've learned to love each and every one of ya, and I thank God for ya, and asks His blessings on y'all."

"Very touching," Jack said, smiling. "Very touching, indeed; but one minute from now, these folks are gonna be so scared of me they'll do whatever they're told. And you, my friend, will be dead."

Jack looked down at his feet searching for something. The scent of death was in the air, making the horse under Malachi skittish.

"Easy girl, easy girl, not yet," Jack said as he petted the horse to calm her down. He again looked to the ground at his feet, searching. Then he found it – a long, thin switch. He ran his hand along it removing the leaves. When it was bare, he stood to one side behind the horse.

"Ready to meet your maker, Pastor?" He brought the hand holding the switch far back behind him. "Hey-ah!" He let the switch fly, hitting the horse on the romp.

Malachi's body tensed, his eyes closed tightly. Howls came from the crowd; the women screamed. The horse galloped forward, leaving Malachi suspended in midair. He dangled from the limb of the tree. It all happened so fast, but not fast enough to break his neck. He slowly strangled as the noose tightened around his neck. The rope burned into his skin. He instinctively kicked like a puppet on a string. His eyes opened wide. He could see the crowd but he couldn't hear them. All he heard was the sound of his blood pulsating in his ears. He could hear his own heartbeat became slower till it was near stopping. The vision of the crowd became blurrier and darker with each second. Then all went black and he lost consciousness.

****

The darkness was all around. Malachi could feel nothing. He couldn't tell up from down. He should have been frantic, but he felt calm. Off in the distance was a golden light. He wasn't sure if the light became bigger, or it came closer, or he came closer to it; but the light was suddenly all around. It was warm and comfortable standing within that light.

A figure walked between him and the light. Malachi could only make out the person's outline, but he could tell it was a man.

The man spoke softly, "Don't be afraid. Have no fear."

It took Malachi a moment to recognize the voice.

"Daddy, is that ya?" Malachi asked.

Malachi stepped forward and reached out for his father.

"You mustn't touch me, son. It's not your time. You'll be goin' back soon. I just wanna tell ya how proud I am of ya. There are so few things a man can wish for his son. That he finds happiness. That he doesn't make the same mistakes. And that he's heaven bound. Are ya happy, son?"

"I haven't thought about it in a long time," Malachi said. "Yes, I am, Daddy. I am happy."

"Good, that's all I wanted to hear. Ya best be goin' back, son. Ya got lots more to do. I love ya, son."

"I love ya, too, Daddy."

With that, everything went black.

****

They all watched in horror as Malachi swung forward and back, his eyes closed, his face growing red and then pale. Suddenly, as if in answer to their prayers, a miracle happened. The branch that held him broke off from the tree. The break was close to the trunk and the branch, the rope, and the unconscious Malachi fell to the ground.

Gun in hand; Jack rushed to stand over Malachi. He aimed at his head, and pulled the trigger. Before the pistol fired, Tom Bennett hit Jack's arm; the gun went off; and the bullet went skyward.

"Tom, have you gone crazy?" Jack shouted.

Tom got right into Jack's face. "No, but I think you have. I told you I didn't like the idea of killing a man of God; but I went along with it. Now, look what's happened. It's providence, Jack. This was an act of God; and I ain't gonna buck him. What part of the sky has to fall on you, Jack, before you realize you're fighting against the powers that be; and you ain't ever gonna win?" Tom turned to the others. "I'm out of here! Who else is with me?"

They turned away; and one by one, they mounted their horses.

"You comin', Jack?" Tom asked, looking down at Bates.

"Y'all fools!" Jack shouted. "If we don't lay down the law now, the South will never rise again."

"Then so be it!" Tom added. "But if you wanna fight the Almighty, you can go right ahead; but we're out of here."

In anger, Jack mounted his horse.

"Blast y'all," said Jack.

The landowners rode off eastward screaming like banshees, leaving a blur of dust behind.

Everyone else ran to Malachi. Percy was the first to him. He took the noose from off his neck, and loosened his collar.

"Back off, everybody; give him some air."

Malachi lay motionless in Percy's arms. The sound of mumbled prayers filled the air. All of a sudden, Malachi stared coughing and wheezing.

"Quick, somebody get him some water."

The next instant, Percy put a tin cup to Malachi's lips and slowly let him drink. Malachi opened his eyes.

"Ya had us scared there for a minute, Pastor. We thought we might have lost ya."

"Help me to my feet," Malachi groaned.

Once standing, Emmanuel pushed his way through the crowd. He rushed to Malachi, wrapped his arms around Malachi's leg and pressed his face against his thigh. The boy was crying franticly.

Malachi took hold of the child and hugged him tightly.

"It's all right, Emmanuel; I'm gonna be just fine."

Malachi straightened up, and the first face he focused on was Woody's. His eye went straight to the handsaw at Woody's side. Then he looked to the ground at the fallen tree branch. The broken edge was smooth. He looked at Woody's handsaw again, and again at the broken branch. Then he looked at Woody.

"Woody, ya didn't...?"

"I hate this tree," Woody said. "I hate it for what it stands for. I think we should chop it down and do something good with it, like cut it into lumber for the new church."

Malachi couldn't help himself. He burst into a fit of laughter, as did Woody. The two men hugged each other, and the crowd joined in the laughter.

A moment later once the laughter died, Malachi became solemn again.

"This won't be the end of it. We've got to come up with a plan."

"But what can we do?" Percy asked.

Malachi looked about at all the scared and worried faces, and then he noticed one face was missing.

"Eli, where's Eli?" Malachi asked.

Bessie, Eli's wife, stepped forward. There were tears in her eyes and she was trembling.

"Bessie," said Malachi, "Where's Eli?"

She pointed to the west. "He's gone yonder to fetch a gun from the Yankee graves. He says he ain't turnin' the other cheek. He swears he's gonna kill 'em all."

Malachi handed Emmanuel to one of the women.

"Women and children, stay here. All able-bodied men come with me. We gotta find Eli and stop him before he gets himself killed."

Eighteen

We Will Understand It By and By

The small group of men led by Malachi and Percy hurried to Eli's home. It was like everyone else's home, just a small run-down shack. As they approached it, Malachi shouted.

"Eli, are ya in there?"

They rushed inside to find no one. Everything seemed in its place.

"Do ya think he had a gun, and he's been here already and gotten it?" Malachi asked.

No one had an answer. Then Arthur Daly, a young man and a good friend of Eli, spoke up.

"There's some Union soldiers buried less then a mile north of here. Eli and I found it about a year ago. The graves are marked with the soldiers' rifles', bayonets stuck in the ground. We said how easy it would be to just take one of the guns for ourselves, but we was too spooked to take one. Maybe that's where Eli's gone."

"Ya think ya could find the spot again?" Malachi asked.

"Sure 'nuff."

They made their way through the forest, Arthur in the lead. Now and then he'd stop to get his bearings and then trudge on. Finally, they came to a small, dark clearing. Arthur stopped in this tracks.

"Is this the place, Arthur?"

"Looks like it."

If it was, the underbrush had grown over the graves and concealed them. Arthur walked about, moving the vines and turf with his foot.

"Here's one," Arthur shouted.

It clearly wasn't freshly dug, but it was a grave. Arthur bent down and came up holding a rifle.

"Here's another one," exclaimed Arthur.

Malachi took the rifle from Arthur and inspected it.

"It's been too long out here; it's useless. Are there any other graves?"

"I remembered there was at least a dozen of them," Arthur replied.

"Everybody spread out and see what ya can find," Malachi said.

The men went about the clearing, moving the underbrush with their feet.

"Here's another," one of the men shouted.

Malachi rushed to him, took the rifle, and inspected it.

"It ain't in good shape; but with a little cleaning, it'd probably work," Malachi proclaimed.

"Pastor Jones, y'all had better come here!" shouted Wilber Gentry.

Wilber was no more than fifteen. He was tall for his age, and wiry. They rushed to his side. He was scared out of his wits. His eyes were wide. His hand shook as he pointed to the ground, and he stammered in fear as he spoke."

They all looked to the ground to where Wilber pointed. There at their feet was an open grave, and next to the grave was the corpse of Union soldier. The body was filthy, incrusted with the dark brown earth. It was in such an advance state of decomposition that it was more a skeleton that a corpse. The clothing that clung to it was now soiled blue rags, hardly recognizable as a uniform.

Malachi got down on one knee, grabbed a handful of soil, and let it slip through his fingers.

"This earth's been freshly dug. It must have been Eli." Malachi stood up. "But why would he do such a horrible thing?"

"Bullets," Percy said, pointing to an empty ammo belt around the dead soldier's waist. "Once he found a rifle that was still good, he needed bullets. It would seem he found them. Eli has a gun and bullets. We need to hurry and find him before he does something foolish."

"I'd like to bury this poor fellow, but time isn't on our side. We'll have to come back," Malachi said.

****

Seeing how Jack and his men rode off going east, it seemed logical to head east. They kept to the roads, looking for hoof prints. There were none.

"This is useless," CJ Billings complained. CJ was a fine young man, a good friend and worker; but everyone knew CJ wasn't one for putting out more effort than he felt necessary to accomplish anything. "They're on horseback, and we're on foot. We'll never catch up with them.

"CJ, don't ya understand? It ain't Jack and his gang we need to find. It's Eli, and he's on foot, just like us," Percy said.

"Maybe if we were someplace up high above all these trees, we could see something?" Malachi stated.

"If we go north, we'll get to higher ground," Woody suggested.

"Let's give it a try," said Malachi.

They turned north, off the road and into the woods. The trees were close and in full bloom, which blocked out the sun. It was dark, making the going slow. At first, the ground was level; but slowly the incline became steep and gradually steeper, till they were climbing almost straight up, clinging to rocks. Near the summit, there were few trees. At the top, they could see off into the horizon in most directions. Still, there were some nearby trees that blocked their view.

"I wish we could see more to the west," Malachi exclaimed.

"I can take care of that," said Mosley Butler. Mosley just turned thirteen. He wasn't quite old enough or big enough to be part of the search party. But in the confusion, he'd tagged along, which was a good thing, as he had one talent none of the others, especially the older men, had.

Mosley sat down on the ground and took off his shoes. He walked up to one of the thinner, taller trees and wrapped his arms around it. With a quick jump, he dug his bare feet into sides of the tree. He started shimming up till he could take hold of the lower branches. From that point, he took hold of one branch after another, getting a foothold, working his way to the top of the tree.

"Mosley can move up and down a tree as fast as most folk can move about on flat ground," Woody said with pride. Mosley was Woody's nephew on his sister's side.

When Mosley reached the top, Malachi cupped his hands at both sides of his mouth and shouted up at the boy.

"Do ya see anything?"

Seated firmly on one of the upper thicker branches, Mosley pointed to the west.

"Fire! Reverend Jones, I see smoke billowing up in the west where the church used to be."

"It could be the women are cooking," Percy pointed out.

Mosley was still able to hear the others below.

"Ain't anybody cooking," Mosley shouted. "The smokes too black and there's too much of it."

"Get yourself down here," shouted Percy. "We need to get back."

The group started down the hill, knowing young Mosley would catch up in time. They stared downward so fast that some of the men tumbled, scraping their hands and knees on the rocks. Some of them got bloody.

When they got to level ground, they ran as fast as they could. They made it back to the road and headed west. When they got to Addie's old shack, they could smell wood burning. As they approached the church area, they could see the smoke spewing over the treetops. Making the turn, they were confronted with the Hanging Tree in flames from the roots to the leaves and the branches at the very top. The fire was so intense they could feel the heat. The women were far from the tree, keeping the crying children safely at bay. The men took hold of large, sharp-edged stones, and dug a furrow around the tree to keep the fire contained. When they finished, the men approached the women and children.

Since Addie's passing, Francine Gumm was the oldest woman in the congregation. Most folk described her as feisty. Francine walked up to Malachi holding one of the other women's babies in her arms.

"Eli, it was Eli who done this. He came running into the clearing like a madman, carrying a can of kerosene. He wouldn't listen to no one, not even Bessie, his wife. He poured the kerosene all over the tree and set it on fire, yelling something about there never gonna be any more hangings. He's got a gun, ya know?"

"Yeah, we know."

Bessie came over to Malachi. "Ya have to stop him, Pastor. He told me he looked for Jack Bates and his men but couldn't find them. He said he was gonna hurt Bates the way he was hurt when they killed Addie. He's determined to go to the Bates farm and kill Mrs. Bates. She's just an old woman, Pastor. Ya gotta hurry."

"Don't ya worry, we'll find him," Malachi said. Then he turned to the other men. "Who knows how to get to the Bates farm?"

"I do," Woody said.

"Then ya can lead the way."

****

It was torment for Eli to watch how they treated Pastor Jones. For the sake of the others, he held back his anger and did nothing. Standing at the back of the crowd, Bessie held tightly to his arm, knowing full well what he was going through. When Jack Bates whipped the horse out from under Pastor Jones leaving him dangling from the rope to slowly die, Bessie dug her nails into her husband's arm, a silent plea for him to be forbearing.

When the tree branch gave way and Pastor Jones fell to the ground, she released her grip. There was a feeling of relief that they all felt. When the landowners rode off, they all ran forward with gratitude in their hearts. But not Eli. He remained angry; and as the others rushed to their pastor, he slowly backed away. When he was out of the clearing, he turned and began running.

He remembered the day he and his friend, Arthur, came on the graves of Union soldiers. There were guns there. He headed for the spot by memory.

When he arrived at the gravesite, it surprised him how much the undergrowth had covered the graves. He muddled about, finding rifles on the ground. Most of them were no longer any good – the seasons had seen to that. But he finally found one, the worse for wear, but still functional.

He was just about to leave the clearing when he realized he had no bullets. He thought of the possibility one of the buried soldiers might have bullets on their person. The thought revolted him, and filled him with shame. To think he would even entertain such a ghoulish idea was not like him. But the anger got the best of him. With a flat rock and his bare hands, he began digging up one of the graves. He felt as if he was standing outside himself watching himself do this strange act. Perhaps the only way his mind could cope with the deed was by disassociating himself from himself.

He dragged the corpse from its grave. He tried not to focus on what he saw, afraid it would drive him mad. He found a handful of bullets and put them in his pocket. His next thought was to rebury the soldier; but then he realized time was of the essence and he needed to hurry.

"I'm sorry, brother, for disturbing your sleep. Please forgive me. If I get out of this alive, I'll be back to put ya to rest," He said, standing over the dead man.

Eli made it through the woods to the road. Since the landowners rode off into the east, he turned eastbound. He kept looking for horse tracks, but found none. Deer and wild boar, but no horse tracks. When he came to the outskirts of the county, he decided to turn back.

That proved to be pointless. There was no sign of Jack Bates and his men. Eli began to run, to make up lost time. Running gave him a desperate and urgent feeling. It washed over him; and with it came confusion. He ran without purpose, save for hatred and anger, not knowing what direction he was headed. He ran till he came on an old shack. He almost laughed when he realized he stood in front of his own home.

The memory of the pastor hanging from the tree flooded his mind, which gave way to visions of all the others who'd been killed that very way at that very tree. His anger was now directed at the tree. He wanted it to not exist, to be no more. He'd destroy it.

He found a half-full can of kerosene with his tools that he always kept in a wood box far from the house. With one hand holding the handle of the kerosene can and the rifle tucked under his other arm, he took off toward the church site.

Eli came rushing out of the woods and into the clearing. His crazed manner and looks scared the women and got the children to crying. He put down the rifle and poured all the kerosene over the trunk of the tree. His wife ran to his side and took hold of his arm. She was crying.

"Eli, darlin', ya mustn't."

"Get back, Bessie."

He took a match from his top pocket, stuck it, and threw it at the tree. The tree's kerosene-soaked trunk caught fire in a flash. Eli picked up the rifle and took hold of his wife as they backed away from the tree.

The flames licked their way up the tree. When they got to the branches, the leaves lit like candles. In no time, the tree was engrossed in red and orange flames. Black smoke rose to the sky.

"I couldn't find Jack and his men," Eli told Bessie.

There was a look on his face that scared her.

"Eli, just forget it all. The pastor's gonna be just fine."

"Will Addie be just fine?" Elis said. "Is Pastor Davis gonna be fine?"

"Eli, darlin', why are ya doin' this?"

"I couldn't find them," Eli repeated. "So I'm gonna hurt him like he hurt us. I wonder how he'd feel if he lost someone near and dear to him? His wife should be home, about now."

Again, in tears, Bessie pleaded with her husband. "Eli, why are ya doin' this?"

"I'm doin' it for you, darlin', and I'm doin' it for me, and for all the others."

"I can't stop ya," Bessie said. "But if you're doin' it for me, don't bother. I won't accept it. I want nothin' to do with it."

"I gotta do this, Bessie; I just gotta," With rifle in hand, Eli turned and ran off out of the clearing.

Eli knew the way to the Bates Plantation like the back of his hand. He was born a slave there. He'd lived all his life there till the war ruined the farms and the slaves scattered.

So much change accrued since he'd last laid eyes on the Bates Plantation. The front gate of iron lay on the ground. The fields were brown and dry. The road up to the main house was full of holes that had collected rainwater.

The main house was dilapidated and looked abandoned. Most of the window panes were missing or cracked, and shutters dangled by a single nail. The white paint was now flaked away and nearly gone, exposing the wooden planks that made up the building.

As he approached slowly, he saw Miss Abby Bates, Jack Bates' wife. She was on the front porch, sitting in her rocking chair. He hardly recognized her; it had been so long since he last saw her. Every strand of hair on her head was now gray. The wrinkles in her face were deep and many. Her hands were boney and covered with spotted skin. A small black boy stood behind her, gently and slowly rocking her. Her eyes were closed; she was sleeping.

There were three steps leading up to the porch, Eli placed his left foot on the middle step. The old wood creaked under his weight, waking her. Her eyes opened and she looked in his direction. It took a moment to clear her vision. When she recognized him, she smiled. Eli kept the rifle pointed down.

"Eli," Miss Abby exclaimed. "It's good to see you. It's been too long."

"Good to see ya, too, Miss Abby," Eli found himself saying.

"Come closer. Let me take a good look at you. My eyes ain't what they once were." Eli stepped up onto the porch and moved near to her. "That's better," she said. "My, you have turned into a fine young man. Are you married?"

"Yes, her name is Bessie."

"Do you have any children?"

"Not yet."

"Oh, they'll come in time; don't you worry."

The old woman moved slowly. She seemed beaten down by the world. She reached out, taking Eli's hand.

"It's so sweet of you, Eli, to come to comfort me in the moment of my grief." Eli looked confused. Miss Abby pointed to the young boy standing behind her. "It was Henry, here, who told me about it. Didn't you, Henry? Why don't you tell Eli all about what you saw?"

The boy stopped pushing the rocking chair. The old woman took hold of him and moved him to the side of the chair.

"It was like this," Henry said. "I was walkin' past the old Parker farm when I heard gunshots. I ran behind a tree. Massa Jack and his men were ridin' their horses hard, like devils they was. Behind them was a whole lot of Yankee soldiers. I don't know who fired on who first; but the Yankees were angry as mad dogs; and they were shooting at the Master and his men. When they got to bein' in front of me, the Yankees shot them dead. I come runnin' here to tell Miss Abby all about it. She ain't takin' it too well." As he spoke the last sentence, he moved his eyes to a side-glance at Miss Abby. This gesture was to indicate to Eli the news had shocked the old woman into a state of denial, had pushed her over the edge.

"You told it well, Henry. You told it just like you told me. First you told it to me, and now to Eli. You sure are a good storyteller. There's a bowl of peaches on the kitchen table. They should be nice and ripe by now. Why don't you go have yourself one and let me have a word with Eli, here? That's a good boy."

"Yes, Miss Abby," Henry said as he left her side and entered the house.

The old woman looked at the rifle under Eli's arm. His hand was on the barrel to keep it steady. She reached out, again, and placed her hand on his.

"Now, Eli, I know you're upset; but violence is not the answer. Leave vengeance to the Lord. Those Yankees will get what's coming to them, in time. I remember your mother. She was a good woman. And I know she taught you better than that. You have to have faith. It's like the old hymn says. Her soft, frail voice went into song.

> *We are tossed and driven on the restless sea of time*
> *Somber skies and howling tempests oft succeed a bright sunshine*
> *In that land of perfect day, when the mist have rolled away*
> *We will understand it by and by*

> *We are often destitute of the things that life demands*
> *Want of food and want of shelter, thirsty hills and barren lands*
> *We are trusting in the Lord, and according to God's word*
> *We will understand it by and by*

> *Trials dark on every hand, and we cannot understand*
> *All the ways that God could lead us to that blessed promise land*
> *But he guides us with his eyes, and we'll follow till we die*
> *For we'll understand it by and by*
> *Temptations, hidden snares often take us unawares*
> *And our hearts are made to bleed for a thoughtless word or deed*
> *And we wonder why the test when we try to do our best*
> *But we'll understand it by and by*

> *By and by, when the morning comes*
> *When the saints of God are gathered home*
> *We'll tell the story how we've overcome*
> *For we'll understand it by and by*

Her tearful eyes looked into his. His grip on the rifle loosened as he searched his heart. Nowhere any longer could he find any anger. He heard a sound behind him. He turned. Standing below was Malachi and the other men.

"No need to worry, Pastor. Everything's all right." He looked to Percy. "Ya need to take some of the men with shovels to the old Parker farm. There are some poor souls needing buryin'." He looked to his friend, Arthur. "Arthur, ya remember that Yankee gravesite we came on about a year ago? Well, I need your help. I need to go there and put to rest a brother of mine." Then he looked to young Mosley. "Mosley, go back to the church and fetch my wife, Bessie. Tell her we be stayin' with Miss Abby for a spell till she be feelin' better."

Nineteen

Not a Word

Malachi woke Emmanuel early. The sun was not yet up. Over breakfast, he gave the boy the day's plan.

"Ya gonna spend the day with CJ and his wife. I've important business, and I won't be home till late tonight. I want ya to behave and do everything you're told. Ya understand?"

Emmanuel nodded.

"Ya need to speak more often," Malachi said. "Now, what do ya say?"

"Yes," said the boy.

"Well, that's good; but you're gonna have to start putting words together, start makin' sentences. Is there anything else ya want to say?"

"No."

"Well, we'll have to work on that," Malachi sighed.

He saw to it the boy was clean and dressed. They walked the half mile to CJ's house.

"Now don't let him get away with anything," Malachi told CJ.

"Oh, no fuss," CJ replied. "Emmanuel is always a good boy." CJ smiled at Emmanuel. "Would ya like to go fishin'?"

"Yes, I would! Thank you!" Emmanuel exclaimed.

"I would? Thank you?" Malachi echoed in amazement. "Why do I only get one-word answers?"

Emmanuel smiled up at him. "I love you."

Those three little words went straight to Malachi's heart. He found it hard to speak.

"I love ya, too. Ya behave yourself; and I'll see ya tonight."

Malachi turned, heading down the road going east, wearing an ear-to-ear grin.

****

Hours later, Malachi stood at the front gate of the Union camp.

"May I help you, sir?" asked the captain of the guards.

Malachi went into his Yankee accent.

"Please tell Colonel Collingsworth that Pastor Jones is here to see him."

The soldier turned and entered the main building only to return a minute or two later.

"The Colonel will see you now, Reverend. Please follow me."

Colonel Collingsworth was not alone in his office; another officer was there. Collingsworth greeted Malachi with a handshake.

"Pastor Jones, good to see you again," Collingsworth motioned to the other officer. "This is Captain Duffy."

"Pleasure to meet you, sir," Malachi said as the two shook hands.

Collingsworth continued, "When I was told you were at the gate, I called for Captain Duffy. I thought it would be a pleasant surprise for both of you." He turned to Captain Duffy. "Reverend Jones is a native of Boston, just like you."

Captain Duffy's face lit up. "Really! This is a pleasant surprise. What part of Boston are you from?"

Again, Malachi was confronted with questions about Boston. He wished he'd never heard of or ever mentioned the city. Malachi never traveled any farther north than Tennessee. He paused for a moment, wondering what to say.

"My father was an architect. We moved to wherever the work was. Not just all over Boston but in the surrounding area. Besides, once I finished seminary, I was sent to work here in the South. I've been here a very long time."

"I would say so," Captain Duffy laughed. "It seems you've picked up some of the local color in your speech. You've acquired a slight Southern accent."

In his nervousness, Malachi had dropped his Yankee speech. He quickly regained it.

"It does seep in when you're exposed to it every day, for as many years as I have," Malachi laughed it off.

"I know what you mean," said Captain Duffy. "As a young man at boarding school I roomed with a fellow from England. Within a year, I'd picked up some of his phrases. You would have thought I was from Liverpool."

The three men laughed. Malachi felt a bit calmer.

"So, Reverend," said Colonel Collingsworth. "Why have you come? Have you found out anything about this Malachi fellow?"

"That is exactly why I'm here, Colonel. I not only found out about Malachi, but there's much afoot since we last met."

"Please continue, Reverend."

"This Malachi is the leader of a group of vigilantes made up of local landowners called the Klan. They go about on horseback at night terrorizing the countryside. They're a frightening group, always dressing in sheets to cover up their identities."

"I've heard about this. It's becoming popular here in the South. It's quite a concern for the Union, especially now that we're approaching the end of the war," Captain Duffy added.

"But does anyone know who this Malachi is?" Colonel Collingsworth asked.

"I've never met him," Malachi said. "But I have been contacted by his followers, this Klan. They showed up at my doorstep with their faces fully covered. They have a plan to help the rebel troops you have imprisoned here escape, and they've asked for my help."

Both Collingsworth and Duffy's interested peaked. Malachi continued to weave his tale.

"They somehow learned that I've been in contact with the prisoners. They have a plan, and they want me to visit the prisoners and tell them of it. In three weeks, the last day of the month, there will be no moon; the night will be at its darkest. That's when they plan to attack."

"One moment, please, Reverend," Collingsworth said as he walked to a place behind his desk. He pointed to a map on the wall. "This is a map of the compound. As you can see, after the front gate we have our barracks and offices. The barracks for the prisoners are behind that in a small open area surrounded by mesh of thick barbed wire, too thick to cut quickly. There are guards at the front gate and at both corners of the barbed wire fence." He pointed at the two corners of the fenced area. "They are our weakest spots. I would image that is where they will attack, especially on a moonless night."

"You would think so," Malachi said, moving closer to the map and pointing to the front gate, "but this Malachi is ruthless and arrogant. He plans to attack with his men after midnight at your front gate. They have explosives. They plan to blow up the front gate, attack your barracks, and then free the prisoners by taking them through the front gate."

"I thank you, Reverend," Colonel Collingsworth said. "With this information, we can be ready for them, and spoil their plans. I will have my troops hide on both sides of the front gate, deep in the woods. When they explode the front gate, we will attack them from both sides and close in on them like a vise."

"They won't be expecting that," Captain Duffy added. "They won't know what hit them."

"One last favor," Collingsworth said. "Since you have the prisoners in your confidence, I need you to tell them of Malachi's plans. Just go along with the plan as if you've never spoken with us."

"Of course, Colonel," Malachi said.

Collingsworth went to his office door, opened it, and spoke to one of the guards.

"Escort Reverend Jones to the prisoners barracks." He held the door for Malachi. "Thank you, again, Reverend."

"Don't mention it," Malachi said as he left the office. "I feel it is my duty."

****

Captain Malory and the men gathered around Malachi. Everyone remained silent till they were sure the guard who had brought Malachi to the prisoner's barracks was gone. They kept a man at the window by the front door as a lookout.

"He's gone," said the lookout.

Everyone gave a sigh of relief.

"So, what's new?" Captain Malory asked Malachi.

"It's a bit complicated; but I'll explain it as best I can," Malachi said. "On the last day of the month, three weeks from today, the night will be moonless. I've convinced Colonel Collingsworth a band of vigilantes are going to attack the front gate, fight their way through the compound, and free all of the prisoners."

"That would be foolishness. They'd never make it," Captain Malory snapped.

"There is no group of vigilantes," Malachi replied. "I just got him to believe there is. And outside of setting off a stick of dynamite at the front gate to confirm his belief, the attack will consist of me and a small group of ex-slaves. We will focus on the two back corners of the compound at the weakest links…the logical points to attack, at the barbed wire fence."

144

"It would take too long to cut through the mesh," Malory said.

"We need to figure a way to knock down the whole fence in one quick swoop," Malachi replied.

"What about the guards at those corners?" Captain Malory asked.

"With it being that dark, and their forces concentrated at the front gate, I believe we can take out the guards quietly and without hurting them."

No one spoke for a long time, each muddling through the plan in their mind.

"I hate to ask this," Captain Malory said. "You've gone far beyond the call of duty for your comrades."

"What's that?" Malachi asked.

"Hopefully, the plan goes off without a hitch. We'll be thirty Confederate soldiers, still in uniform, without any food or supplies, not knowing where we are, or how to get to where we want to go."

Malachi thought for moment.

"We don't have much of anything, but I'll try to get ya food and clothing. I'll do my best."

"The guard is comin'," said the lookout.

A moment later, the guard entered the barracks.

"I'm sorry to bother you, Reverend, but your time is up."

"Very well, Sergeant; just give me one more minute."

The guard remained at the door. Malachi stood at the front of the room and addressed them all in his finest Northern accent.

"I pray that the Lord bless and keep all of you. Before I leave, let us lift our voices once more in song."

Malachi began to sing. After the first line, the men recognized the song and they all joined in.

Dey crucified my Lord
And he never said a mumblin' word
Not a word, not a word, not a word

Dey nailed him to the tree
And he never said a mumblin' word
Not a word, not a word, not a word

Dey pierced his side
And he never said a mumblin' word
Not a word, not a word, not a word

De blood came tricklin' down
And he never said a mumblin' word

Michael Edwin Q.

Not a word, not a word, not a word

He bowed his head and died
And he never said a mumblin' word
Not a word, not a word, not a word

Dey crucified my Lord
And he never said a mumblin' word
Not a word, not a word, not a word.

Twenty

We Stand at Last

Every living soul has a talent. Woody's talent was the ability to picture something in his mind and make it real. Whatever he imagined, he could give life to it in wood. Where some folks see only a tree, Woody saw a church. What Michelangelo did with stone and pigment, Woody could do with timber. He'd fell the tree and cut and shave it into perfect strips of lumber. He laid all the different size beams where he wanted them for easy access.

No one questioned his method. The blueprint was in Woody's head, and everyone trusted his vision. They knew that if they followed his instructions without question, they'd be rewarded with a church they'd be proud of.

"This church is gonna be bigger and better than the last one," Woody claimed.

No one had any doubt it would be better, but some questioned why it had to be bigger.

"We need to have room to grow," said Woody. "We're gonna build us a church that will last for generations, for our children's children. And that'll mean more folks. And as for children, I don't know 'bout y'all; but I plan to have a few more before my day is done and they plant me."

Woody measured out the length and width of the building with string, which he tied to pegs he'd hammered into the ground. Then they cleared and leveled the ground within that perimeter.

They dug and pounded beams into the earth, making sure they were all the same height, and then connected them all with crossbeams. Upon this they placed a base that the floor would rest on. After that, it was the slow process of fastening one piece to another. At first, it looked as if it would never make any sense. But in time, it began to look like the vision that was inside Woody's head.

Everyone worked hard. Even the children pulled their weight. But no one worked harder than Malachi. He was so excited about the new building that he could hardly contain his enthusiasm. He slept little at night, writing out sermons and preparing himself for the new building.

Some of the folks worked on the pews and the pulpit while the others worked on the building. There was no glass for the windows; that would come in time. The sound of saws and hammers could be heard for a mile. Sunday service was praise and worship only, no sermon, as to get back to the task at hand. All minds were focused on that day. And when it came, it was glorious.

They entered the new building, and it felt holy. They moved about admiring their own handy work.

"Don't sit down in the pews yet; the paint won't be dry for another day," Woody warned.

Percy noticed Malachi admiring the new pulpit.

"Go ahead, Pastor," Percy said. "Try her on for size."

"Yes! Yes!" the others shouted as they applauded.

Just then, the sound of horse hooves could be heard, along with the creak of wagon wheels. The congregation went silent. Some looked out the pane-less windows to see who was approaching. They had no idea who it could be. No one in the congregation owned a horse, let alone a wagon.

"It's Eli, and he's driving a wagon," someone shouted. "Bessie's with him; and there's someone else with them. It's a white woman. It's....Miss Abby!"

They waited silently to hear their footsteps on the wooden steps at the church front. Eli was the first to enter, followed by his wife who helped the old woman move forward.

"We wouldn't miss this for the world," Eli said as the three made their way to the front of the church.

"It looks wonderful," Bessie commented.

"Glad y'all could make it," Malachi said. He bowed slightly to the old woman. "Good to see ya, Miss Abby. How ya been feelin'?"

The old woman smiled. She stepped forward and pointed to a place behind the pulpit. "You folks don't have an organ, yet." She turned to Bessie. "Remind me to speak to my husband, Mr. Bates, about the matter. Jack donated the organ for the last church; I'm sure he'd be glad to donate another one. Don't forget to remind me, Bessie."

"I won't," Bessie said, knowing all too well, as well as the others, that Jack Bates no longer existed, except within the confines of Miss Abby's mind.

"We were just about to dedicate the new church," Malachi said to Eli.

"We'll, don't stop on our account," Eli replied with a smile."

In that moment, Malachi looked deep into Eli's eyes. All the anger that once lived there was gone. Eli's eyes were bright, calm, and caring. Malachi smiled at Eli and gave his arm a grip of reassurance and pride.

Malachi stepped up to the pulpit and smiled at all the happy faces looking up at him. Then he looked upwards.

"Dear Lord, look down on your children this day and see how we smile. We thank ya for all you've done for us. We thank ya for Woody whose skill and know-how guided us."

"Amen! Amen!" voices cried through the crowd.

Malachi continued. "We thank ya for the strength to see us through this and for providing us with the materials needed. We give ya praise and thanksgiving. We ask that ya bless this building and all who labor on it and all who enter it. May it be a place of great joy, a place where many souls are saved. May we see many weddings, and births, and only the deaths of those well used up, tired, and ready. May it be a place you'd be proud to call home. All God's children said..."

"Amen," they shouted to the rafters.

A Slave's Song

Malachi turned to his left to the empty space that would be a perfect place for a church organ. Then he thought of Addie. He could picture her pounding on the keys of the organ and singing louder than anyone else. He went into song and everyone joined in.

Lift every voice and sing till earth and heaven ring
Ring with the harmonies of Liberty
Let our rejoicing rise, high as the list'ning sky
Let it resound loud as the rolling sea
Sing a song full of faith that the dark past has taught us
Sing a song full of hope that the present has brought us
Facing the rising sun of a new day begun
Let us march till victory is won

Stony the road we trod, bitter the chast'ning rod
Felt in the days when hope unborn has died
Yet with a steady beat, have not our weary feet
Come to the place for which our fathers sighed
We have come over a way that with tears have been watered
We have come, treading our path thro' the blood
Of the slaughtered
Out of the gloomy past, till now we stand at last
Where the white gleam of our bright star is cast

God of our weary years, God of our silent tears
Thou who hast brought thus far on the way
Thou who hast by Thy might, led us into the light
Keep us forever in the path, we pray
Lest our feet stray from the places, our God, where we met thee
Lest our hearts, drunk with the wine of the world, we forget thee
Shadowed beneath thy hand, may we forever stand
True to our God, true to our native land

The last note hummed for a moment in the air. It never died and faded, but was absorbed into the timbers and the rafters of the building. And the church became theirs and they became the church.

Malachi waited a moment before speaking; and when he did, he spoke softly.

"I have something to ask y'all; and I feel we are close enough for me to ask. What I want to ask y'all isn't fair. All of ya have given and sacrificed so much already. But I'm goin' to ask ya to consider givin' some more.

"Like every one of ya, I, too, have a past. I've traveled many a strange road to get here. I grew up on my daddy's farm. Worked the land from when I was a little fella till I became a man. At that time, I was drafted into the army...the Confederate Army."

Malachi waited for a response. There was none.

"If y'all no longer want me for your pastor, I will understand."

Percy stepped forward and addressed the congregation.

"As ya said, Pastor, we all have a past. I may not agree with your past; but I know the man who stands before us. We've listen to ya preach. We've lived and worked alongside ya. I don't know what ya was; I know what ya is. I'm pleased and proud to call ya pastor. If anyone else don't feel that way, ya best speak up."

Percy waited. No one responded.

"Go ahead, Pastor," Percy said. "Ya were gonna ask a favor of us."

Clearly, Malachi was moved by the gesture of confidence he received from his congregation. He took a moment to regain his composure.

"As y'all know, there is a Yankee camp not far from here where they keep prisoners of war locked up. Those were comrades of mine, my friends. They yearn to escape and be set free. I promised them I'd help them, and I'll need your help to do it."

"Pastor, are ya askin' us to help ya spring a bunch of Johnny Rebs out of prison?" Francine Gumm asked. "Why would we do that?"

"These men are good men," Malachi said. "They just want to go home to their families. I have their word they will give up the fight and just go home."

"And ya trust them?" CJ Billings asked.

"With my life," Malachi said.

"I don't understand," said CJ. "We've suffered under slavery all our lives. Now that things look like they're gonna turn around, ya want us to reward the men who fought to keep us in slavery?"

"Not reward," said Malachi. "I'm askin' ya to show mercy."

"Mercy?" CJ laughed. "Why should we show mercy?"

"Because that's what we do," Eli said, stepping forward. "Are we not a church? Didn't the Lord say to love your enemies? If these men are willin' to give up the fight, then I say we help them. Because that's what we're called to do."

Again, there was a moment of silence.

"Looks like ya got our help, Pastor," Percy said. "Now, how ya plan to do this?"

"I've convinced the Commander of the post that they will be attacked on the last night of the month, when the moon is dark. He believes a group of vigilantes will attack the front gate. But while they're guarding the front gate, we will subdue the guards at the other end where there's nothing but barbed wire."

"But if we overcome the guards and tear down the fence, unless we kill the guards, they'll be able to identify us," CJ questioned. "I mean, a group of black men helping Johnny Rebs escape is memorable. They'll be comin' around here in no time."

"They won't know it's a group of black men," Malachi said. "We're all gonna be wearing white sheets."

"Like the Klan wear," Percy added.

"They'll think we're the Klan, a bunch of white men," Malachi said.

Laughter filled the room, making the mood lighter.

"There is one other thing," Malachi said. "These men will need supplies, if they're gonna escape. They'll need maps, new clothes, and food."

"No offence, Pastor" said Francine Gumm. "Ya asked us for Christian charity, which we've agreed to give. But there is a point where ya can give till ya bleed. I myself will be glad to sit down and draw out some maps. But as for clothing, there ain't any to be had or given. And as for food, there's ain't much to go around for us here. I'm sure ya agree, as we all do, we can't take from our children's mouths to give to unfortunate men. I will give till it hurts, but not at the expense of the babies."

"Perhaps, I can be of help."

They all turned to see who spoke. It was Miss Abby.

"There is everything you need in the barn at the Bates farm. There is enough food for your friends, your children, and everyone else there, and still have some left over. As for clothing, there are stacks of work clothes, enough to share and to keep."

Everyone looked at the old woman with astonished and questioning expressions.

"She's tellin' ya the truth," Eli said. "I've seen it. There are supplies of all kinds needed to get us all on our feet. Most important, there are sacks of seed, food for the future."

"And I give it all to you," Miss Abby said, "on one condition."

"What is that?" Malachi asked.

"That you allow me to be part of your church."

"My good lady," Malachi said, "the only thing ya need to be a part of this church is to simply ask. We take ya in for the asking with open arms."

"Well, in that case," Miss Abby said, "I give these things to you all because I'm a member of this church."

"Bless ya, Miss Abby," Malachi said.

"It's my pleasure," said the old woman. She looked at Bessie. "Bessie, don't forget. When we get home, I need to ask my husband, Jack, if he'd be willin' to donate another church organ. I'm sure he will. He's a fine man."

They all walked Miss Abby out to the wagon. One by one they thanked her.

Eli slapped the reins, and the wagon took off.

"See ya next Sunday," they called out as the old woman turned to smile and wave goodbye.

Twenty-One

Stand By Me

It was as Miss Abby said. The barn at the Bates farm was filled to the rafters with farm equipment, grains, seeds, clothing, and dry goods.

"There's enough here to get this farm back on its feet," Percy said.

"Then maybe that's what we should to," Malachi said. "It would do the widow Bates a world of good, and everyone else."

"Only this time we work the land for ourselves, as free men," Percy added with a smile.

They took thirty empty grain sacks and filled them with clothing and provisions and placed them in the back of the one-horse wagon. These they would give to the escaped Johnny Rebs.

Eli, who knew the surrounding land better than anyone else, took pen to paper and drew a map with as much detail as he could muster. They held a meeting of some of the more artistic and steady-handed folks at the church. There, they carefully made copies of Eli's map.

"I can't tell the original from the copies," Malachi said in praise. "Great work, y'all."

Most of the artists were the younger folks. They beamed with pride at their pastor's words. It gave them a better sense of being part of the church. In fact, a strong feeling of community grew between everyone in the congregation as each person did what they could.

Everyone decided that only six men would go on the escape mission. Malachi would be the leader. Percy would drive the wagon. Eli would toss the lit sticks of dynamite, which they found in the Bates barn, at the front of the Yankee compound, as a diversion. Being the strongest, Jacob and Isaac Whittle, Percy's sons, would overtake the guards at the back fence. Then they would uproot the corner post of the fence by attaching a chain to the wagon and pulling the post out of the ground. This part of the plan would be under Woody's supervision, assisted by Malachi.

Miss Abby held a sewing circle in her home with some of the ladies of the church. They're job was to take some old sheets and make Klan uniforms for Jacob and Isaac. The headdresses were fitted with holes for the eyes, and the white gowns covered their bodies down to the floor. Only, there was still one major setback.

"Pastor Jones, we've finished the Klan outfits," Bessie said. "Ya need to step inside and have a look-see. We got ourselves a problem."

Malachi stood in the living room of the Bates home. Miss Abby and all the ladies who helped with the sewing were there. Jacob and Isaac stood in the center of the room, modeling their Klan costumes. They looked frightening.

Malachi walked one time around the two young men. "They look fine to me," Malachi said. "What's the problem?"

Jacob and Isaac lifted their hands.

"Oh, I see," Malachi exclaimed.

Their large hands were clearly black, set off more so by the snow-white Klan costumes.

"Do we have any gloves?" Malachi asked.

"I own a pair," Miss Abby said, "but nothing that would fit these two."

"Well, it maybe too dark to notice," Malachi stated.

"We can't take that chance," Bessie said. "If they know that black folk were a part of this, we'll be the first place they'll come lookin'.'"

Malachi thought long and hard.

"Make another costume for me. I'll go with them and make sure it's my hands they see."

Miss Abby grabbed a tape measure and took Malachi measurements, as Bessie wrote them down.

"Consider it done, Reverend," Miss Abby said.

"Now, if y'all excuse me," Malachi said. "I've gotta check on some dynamite."

Eli was inserting a fuse into the six sticks of dynamite he'd lashed together, when Malachi approached him in the barn.

"So, Eli, ya sure ya know what you're doin'?' Malachi asked.

"I've done this dozens of times," Eli responded. "Whenever we cleared land, we needed to blow up tree stumps."

"Yeah, but did ya do it with six sticks of dynamite? It seems a little excessive, don't ya think?"

"Same rules apply," Elis said, "just six times more."

Somehow this didn't comfort Malachi.

****

On the last day of the month, in the late evening, the congregation gathered at the church to see off the six brave men. Everyone laughed and joked, doing their best to ignore the true dangers of such a mission. They ate together, as if it were a church picnic, till the hour became so late that the children began falling asleep where they sat.

The wagon was loaded and ready to go. Before setting off, Malachi stood before the congregation and asked for a blessing.

"Dear Lord, we ask your blessings on our endeavors of this night. Keep us safe from harm and see that no one is hurt, be they enemy or friend. Let us be successful and return to our homes. Amen!"

"Amen," said all.

Malachi ended with a hymn, which they all joined in.

In the midst of tribulation
Stand by me
In the midst of tribulation
Stand by me

Michael Edwin Q.

When the host of hell assail
And my strength begins to fail
Thou who never lost a battle
Stand by me
In the midst of fault and failures
Stand by me
In the midst of fault and failures
Stand by me
When I do the best I can
And my friends don't understand
Thou who knowest all about me
Stand by me

When I'm growing old and feeble
Stand by me
When I'm growing old and feeble
Stand by me
When life becomes a burden
And I'm nearing chilling Jordon
Oh thou "Lilly of the Valley"
Stand by me

The congregation continued to sing as the six men chosen for the mission said their goodbyes to friend and family.

Malachi found Emmanuel asleep in the lap of Francine Gumm, her arms around the child, his head against her breast. Malachi bent low and kissed Emmanuel's forehead.

"Put the boy to bed. I'll be home in the mornin' to make him breakfast," Malachi told Francine. "But if I don't make it back, see that he's well cared for."

"No need to talk such a way," Francine said. "You'll be home in the mornin'. I just know it."

Malachi joined the other five men, and hopped onto the wagon. Eli slapped the reins, and they started off down the road going east. As they made the turn out of sight, they could still hear the congregation singing.

When the storm of life is raging
Stand by me
When the storm of life is raging
Stand by me
When the world is tossing me
Like a ship upon the sea
Thou who rulest wind and water
Stand by me

154

Twenty-Two

My Lonesome Valley

The road was difficult and slow. It was so dark. The night sky, though moonless, was clear, so they followed the stars. There was a feeling of awkwardness as the sound of the horse's hooves and the creak of the wagon's wheels pierced the night's silence. They felt like intruders in God's world.

"Pastor, I've got a question," Jacob said. "Is it right for a man to be scared?"

It was Percy who answered Jacob. Malachi remained silent; as it only seemed fitting the father should guide the son in such matters.

"Why, are ya scared?" Percy asked.

"Yes, I am," Jacob replied.

"And you, Isaac, are ya scared too?" Percy asked.

"Yes, Papa," Isaac admitted in a timid voice.

"That's good," Percy exclaimed. "That tells me I didn't raise no fools. Only a fool has no fear. Fear is intelligence. It lurks in the body and pops its head whenever it's needed. But a man ain't just a body; he's a spirit too. And that's where his courage lies. That's what makes a man a man: when he can dig deep into his soul and pull out enough courage to push aside his fear. The fear ain't gone; it's just put aside. Ya understand what I'm sayin' to ya, son?"

"I think I do, Papa," Isaac said. "But it ain't easy; it's hard."

"I ain't never known anything worth its salt that was," Percy relied. "But some things is worth it."

No one spoke for a long time, each of them quietly pondering what was just said.

They continued to travel eastward till they got to the top of a hill. There, off in the distance, they saw the lights of the compound on the flatlands ahead.

"There she is," Eli pointed out. "Everybody get ready."

Fifteen minutes later, they were at the edge of the forest looking out at the field where the compound lay. They stopped the wagon. Jacob, Isaac, and Malachi changed into their Klan outfits. They made sure they had enough rope to tie up the guards. Eli double-checked his bundle of dynamite. Percy and Woody would remain with the wagon.

Jacob, Isaac, and Malachi started off to the far end of the field by following the edge of the forest. They would go to the far end of the compound and subdue the first guard. Eli did the same, following the edge of the forest, only he went in the opposite direction till he was at the front gate of the compound.

****

There wasn't a single Yankee soul left on the compound. There wasn't even a guard at the front gate. Colonel Collingsworth separated his men into two equal platoons. One hid in the forest to the right of the compound; the other half waited in the forest to the left of the compound. After the prisoners, who did not suspect Collingsworth's plans, were fed their evening meal, he marched his troops into their positions. Not knowing the exact time of the attack, they waited in the dark, keeping low and silent. Under orders that any soldiers who broke rank or spoke would be punished severely, they remained quiet and motionless.

Colonel Collingsworth was with his men. The plan was to rush the enemy from both sides as they attached the front gate. They waited patiently for the initial blast brought on the front gate, which they presumed would come in the form of a small cannon shot. Little did they know the blast would be nothing more than a half dozen sticks of dynamite, lit and thrown at the front gate by only one very frightened young man.

Knowing the plan in advance, when Eli came to a certain point, he walked deeper into the woods so he could go around the platoon. Even in the dark he could see the backs of their heads as they crouched down behind rocks and logs. When he was directly in front of the compound, but too far to toss the dynamite, he got down low, inching his way toward the front gate. When he was an arms-throw from the compound, he hunkered down behind a large rock. He waited, giving Malachi and the Whittle brothers time to subdue the guards at the back end of the compound.

****

After dinner, the tension in the prisoner's barracks began to mount. They thought it strange that no matter what window they looked out they never saw one Yankee guard. The atmosphere was quiet, but nervous.

"It'll be dark soon," said Sergeant Hastings. "Once the sun is down maybe we should go to the fence and wait?"

"No, we need to stay here and wait," Captain Malory warned. "We need to give Malachi time to overtake the guards at the fence; but we need to be out of the barracks before the explosion at the front gate. Malachi said he'd give us a signal."

"What's the signal?" Hastings asked.

"I don't know. Malachi said we'd know it when we heard it. In the meantime, we need to have the men act as if this were any other night."

"What for?" said Hastings. "Have ya looked outside? There ain't a guard to be found."

"Doesn't matter," said the Captain. "Ya never know who might be around. Besides, if the men stay busy, it'll keep their minds off of what's to come, Stop 'em from bein' nervous. And it'll make the time go quicker."

"Whatever ya say, Captain." Hastings addressed the men. "All right, you bums, how about a game of cards?"

****

156

Malachi and the Whittle brothers hid behind a bush at the edge of the woods, watching the guard march up and down his post at the far corner of the back fence.

"When he gets to the corner and turns to march down the length of the fence, let's make a run for him. The two of ya grab him from behind and tie his hands and his legs. I'll get him from the front and gag him. Whatever ya do, try not to hurt him."

They waited and watched, counting how many steps the guard took in each direction and how long it took for him to complete a full cycle.

"Get ready," Malachi whispered. "Try to make as little noise as possible. Ready...and...go!"

Keeping low, they rushed out of the woods, across the field, sneaking up behind the guard. The two large brothers were on him and in no time had him on the ground. They began to tie his hands behind him and his legs together. Malachi approached him from the front and placed his hand over his mouth.

The soldier was a young boy still in his teens. His eyes went wild. He was visibly too frightened to think clearly and put up a fight.

"Don't worry. We ain't gonna hurt ya, unless ya do something stupid. Open your mouth...wide."

The soldier obeyed without a sound. Malachi placed a handkerchief into the boy's mouth, making sure he saw the white of his hand. They rolled him over onto his stomach. They hogtied him, his tied hands bound to his tied feet. He wasn't going any place soon.

"Now ya be a good boy and just lie here and don't make a sound," Malachi said as he picked up the boy's rifle that was on the ground.

He motioned for his companions to follow him. Still keeping low, they ran along the fence to the far post. When they were close enough to see the other guard marching along the fence, they hit the ground and waited and watched. When the soldier was marching with his back to them, they rushed him. Malachi took the rifle he was carrying and shoved it into the soldier's ribs from behind.

"Don't move," Malachi ordered in a low grunt. The guard stopped. "Now, drop your gun and put your hands behind ya."

Isaac and Jacob came up behind the soldier and started to tie his hands and feet. Malachi stepped in front of him and pointed the rifle at his gut.

"Now, just do as you're told and ya won't get hurt."

This soldier was much older than the other, with a full beard and crow's feet around the eyes.

"Open your mouth wide," Malachi said, and then he placed a handkerchief into the man's mouth, again making sure the white of his hands were seen.

They placed him facedown on the ground and hogtied him like the other soldier. They made sure he was far from the corner post of the fence. Malachi took another handkerchief and blindfolded his eyes.

Malachi bent low and whispered in his ear. "When they ask ya who did this to ya, tell 'em it was Malachi."

Malachi moved close to the fence, reached into his pocket, pulled out his mouth harp, and started to play. The music traveled through the night air to the barracks only a few yards away.

Inside the barracks, Captain Malory and Sergeant Hastings stood by the back window.

"Hush, everybody," ordered Captain Malory. The men fell silent and listened. "That's Malachi's harp playin'. I'd know it anywhere."

"What song is that?" Sergeant Hastings asked.

"Ya really do have a tin ear, don't ya?" replied Malory. "That's 'Dixie'...the all-clear." He rushed to the door and turned to the others. "Come on, men. We're gettin' out of here."

He swung the door open and rushed out; the others followed him. They ran across the clearing to the corner post of the fence. Malachi was waiting there. He and the other two had taken off their Klan costumes.

"Malachi," Malory shouted. "Ya made it."

"We ain't out of the woods yet," Malachi said. "Just stay calm. We have to wait for the explosion. It should be any minute."

****

Percy, along with Woody, drove the wagon out of the woods and across the clearing. It being so dark, it was difficult to see where he was going. Percy just aimed the horse toward the lights coming from the barracks in the middle of the clearing.

As they came closer, they could make out silhouettes. The white sheets that Malachi and his sons wore, Malachi waved them like a signal flag. They saw them, the tied-up Yankee soldier, and behind the barbed wire fence, the thirty prisoners waiting anxiously.

Percy turned the wagon around and backed it slowly toward the fence.

"Whoa," Malachi whispered, when the back of the wagon was no more than three feet away from the fence.

Woody jumped from the wagon. He took a long heavy chain from the back of the wagon. He wrapped one end of the chain around the large corner post of the fence. Then he lay on the ground and wrapped the other end around the back axle of the wagon. Meanwhile, Malachi took hold of the tied-up Yankee guard and pulled him across the high grass to place him even farther away from any possible danger.

When Woody finished, everyone remained standing quietly in place, waiting to move into action the moment of the explosion. There was a feeling of uneasiness as long minutes passed with not a sound from the front of the compound.

"What could be takin' him so long?" Percy whispered to Malachi. "Ya think maybe he got caught?"

"I doubt it," Malachi said. "If they caught a man with six sticks of dynamite, I'm sure we'd hear some kind of ruckus."

Percy shook his head. "It's just takin' too long. I tell ya, something's not right."

****

The back of the compound wasn't the only place where tension was felt and nerves were on edge. Colonel Collingsworth stood with his officers; now and then he or one of the others would look at their pocket watch.

"It's getting mighty late, Colonel," Captain Duffy whispered. "Do you think they might not be coming?"

"Oh, they're coming all right," Collingsworth replied. "I figured they'd try something in the late hour after midnight. They're sure to attack when they believe we'd be asleep. Catch us with our pants down, so to speak."

"But the men are getting tired and restless, sir," Duffy said.

"This is the Army, Captain," Collingsworth snapped, "not a boy's camp. We're on an important mission. I'll shoot any man I catch sleeping. You understand me, Captain?

"Yes, sir."

****

Eli checked all his pockets twice. He had no matches to light the dynamite. If he could, he would have kicked himself for being so unprepared. He'd waited long enough for his comrades to perform their part of the plan. Surely, by now, the guards at the far end of the compound were overtaken and hogtied. He could picture them in his mind standing at the post of the fence with the prisoners on the other side of the fence waiting for an explosion that was to be their diversion. What was he to do?

He thought hard but not for long, he didn't have that luxury. He had to do something. He had to take a chance, even if it meant his life. Leaving the dynamite on the ground and getting down as low as possible; he crawled to his left into the darkness.

After a few yards, he could make out the figures of a group of Yankee soldiers hunkering down behind shrubs and rocks. He took the long way around and came up on them, but remained hidden behind a large rock.

"Hey, ya got a match?" Eli whispered.

"Smithy, is that you?" the soldier on the other side of the rock whispered back.

"Yeah, it's me. Ya got a match?" Eli said softly.

"Are you crazy?" replied the soldier. "Get caught smoking, Collingsworth will have you shot."

"Don't worry about me. I'm gonna go deep in the woods to smoke. Just give me a match."

Eli heard the soldier rummaging through his coat pocket, and then a hand appeared from around the rock holding a match. Eli was just about to take it when he realized the man's hand holding the match was bright white, which reminded him of how dark his hands were.

"I can't reach it," said Eli. "Toss it over."

With a quick flip of the wrist, the match landed at Eli's feet. He picked it up.

"Thanks," said Eli.

"Do me a favor," said the soldier. "If you get caught, I had nothing to do with it. You hear?"

"Not a word," said Eli as he drew back down and crawled away.

It took him a few minutes to get back to the dynamite. He was sure the others were worried about him and wondering if the explosion would ever happen.

He double-checked the dynamite and the fuse. Having only one match, there'd be no room for mistakes.

He carefully ran the head of the match against the surface of a rock. It immediately burst into a large yellow-orange flame. Holding the match in one hand and the dynamite in the other, he brought the match to the fuse. As he did, the flame grew smaller and nearly went out. He held his hand as steady as he could, silently praying the small flame would grow. When it did, he brought the fuse to the match. Inwardly, he began to panic when it wouldn't light. All of sudden, the fuse took to the flame and began to sparkle. He held the dynamite in his right hand, ready to throw it as soon as the fuse was short.

"Look! Do you see that?" someone shouted from the darkness.

"O'Malley, take two men and check it out," he heard another voice say.

Eli could hear the sound of footsteps rustling through the leaves on the ground. When they were close enough to make out their silhouettes, Eli threw the sticks of dynamite at the compound. The fuse was still too long; the dynamite just rolled up against the front gate and lay there.

Eli jumped to his feet and started running into the deep woods. They began to shoot at him. The first few shots missed and hit the trees around him, sending pieces of bark in all directions. The next volley of bullets was much closer. One whizzed past his head. He brought his hand up to his ear. He felt blood. The bullet had sliced it in two. When he let his arm back down, a bullet struck him in the shoulder. He took hold of his arm with his opposite hand. He felt the wetness of the blood. Then a bullet found him in his left thigh. He fell to the ground, but he quickly struggled to his feet. The pain was coming on him. The burning pain in his leg worsened with each footstep. He was still able to run, but at a slow pace. They were sure to catch him.

Just when he was sure all was lost, the explosion happened. He felt the pressure of the blast push him forward and the heat against the back of his neck. He continued to hobble into the woods, not looking back. When he felt it was safe, he got behind a large tree and looked back. The soldiers were running in the opposite direction, heading back to the compound.

****

Colonel Collingsworth looked at his pocket watch. It was far passed midnight. Immediately after putting it back in his pocket, there was shouting. A platoon leader came rushing to him.

"What is it, Sergeant?" Collingsworth asked.

"Someone's seen something," replied the Sergeant.

"Well, don't just stand there. Find out what it is," Collingsworth ordered.

The Sergeant ran off. There was more shouting. They saw something tossed at the compound. The lit fuse shown brightly in the night; it rested on the ground close to the front gate. The next moment, there was the sound of gunfire off in the distance. Before Collingsworth could make an assessment of the situation, Captain Duffy ran into the open and toward the front gate with the intention of putting the fuse out. But it was impossible to know how much time was left.

"Duffy, get back here! Don't be a fool!" Colonel Collingsworth shouted.

But it was too late. The dynamite exploded. The force of the blast knocked Duffy three feet off the ground and four feet back. He staggered to his feet. He was badly shaken but not hurt, which was far better than the front gate and the front portion of the compound had faired.

Malachi's fears were confirmed. Six sticks of dynamite were overkill. The front gate exploded into thousands of tiny flaming splinters that flew in every direction. All the surrounding trees caught fire. In the compound, the offices and Yankee barracks went up in flames. The prisoners' barracks caught on fire. The entire area was ablaze with orange and yellow flames; the heat was intense.

Colonel Collingsworth gave the order for the bugler to blow charge. The soldiers came out from hiding and charged for the front gate from both sides. Collingsworth stood with his men facing the woods, ready to defend the compound, to make a stand against the enemy, prepared to withstand the attack that would never come.

The soldiers who ran after Eli now came rushing back.

"Did you see anyone out there?" Collingsworth asked them.

"Just one man, sir. We winged him, sir."

"It seems we've been duped, sir," said one of the officers standing next to Collingsworth.

"It would seem so," replied Collingsworth. "I fear we've underestimated this Malachi fellow.

There was nothing left to do but try to put out the fire; except the only water available was within the compound, which was up in flames. The soldiers took their shovels and tossed dirt at the fire, which was slow going, but it worked. Others shoveled around the burning trees, trying to contain the fire.

The officer standing next to Collingsworth pointed at the prisoner's barracks that were now fully engulfed in flames. "What about the prisoners, sir?"

Collingsworth looked and shook his head. "Too late for them, I'm afraid. May the Lord have mercy on their souls."

****

"Go!" Malachi shouted as soon as they heard the explosion.

Percy slapped the reins, and the horse took off. But as soon as the slack in the chain was taken up between the wagon and the fencepost, the wagon came to a halt. The thick wooden post tilted forward, but only a few inches. It must have been buried deep in the ground. The horse whinnied with frustration as it strained in vain to go forward.

Jacob and Isaac took hold of the chain and pulled with all their might. Seeing this, Malachi and Woody took hold of the chain to help them. The post leaned forward a few more inches.

"Don't just stand there!" Captain Malory shouted. "Let's lend them a hand."

The prisoners placed their hands on the post and pushed forward. Those who couldn't get their hands on the post pushed the men in front of them.

"Put your backs into it, men," shouted Malory.

They pulled and pushed, sweating and grunting. To every ones surprise, the post could not be uprooted; but it did begin to crack. They could hear the wood creaking, which made them work all the harder.

In a split second, the post snapped like a twig. Luckily, it broke near the bottom. They were able to force the barbed wire fence flat to the ground. The men walked over it into the clearing, into freedom.

Woody went under the wagon and unraveled the chain free from the axle.

"We can't stay here," Malachi warned Captain Malory. "We need to make it to the woods."

"Everyone to the trees, double-time," Malory ordered.

Percy took off for the woods with the wagon, with the men running behind. It was too dark to see where they were going so they followed the rumbling of the wagon.

At the tree line, Percy trudged into the woods till he came to the road. The men came up and halted behind the wagon, all of them out of breath and panting.

Malachi and the two brothers were carrying their Klan costumes, and then they tossed them into the bushes.

Malachi found Captain Malory. He pointed to the back of the wagon. "There are thirty sacks here. Each one contains a change of clothes, a couple of day's food, and a map of the area."

"Ya heard the man," Malory shouted. "Everybody, grab ya a sack."

Jacob and Isaac handed out the sacks to the men. When they finished, Captain Malory gave his farewell speech.

"There's no need to tell ya that time is of the essence so I'm gonna make this short. I'd go east for a spell before I headed south if I were y'all. Maybe even take a northern trail for a bit. I just want y'all to know it's been a privilege to serve with and know each and every one of y'all. And if you're ever in South Georgia, ya got a place to stay. Now get along, good luck, and Godspeed."

Each of them said their quick goodbyes, "Good luck, Captain"; "So long, Captain"; "God bless ya, Captain."

With that, they turned, walk away, and scattered into the darkness.

Just then, a figure came limping out of the dark. It was Eli.

"Eli, are ya all right?" Malachi asked, taking hold of Eli.

"I'll live; but I sure am hurtin'."

"Well, here, get into the wagon."

Woody helped Eli into the back of the wagon and got in beside him. Malachi looked at Isaac and Jacob.

"Best get in the wagon," he said softly. "There's no time to waste."

The two brothers jumped up into the wagon and sat next to Eli.

"Ya wanna sit up front with me, Pastor?" Percy called back.

"No. Y'all go ahead. I got some things I need to discuss with the Captain here."

"But, Pastor..."

"Don't worry about me. Y'all go on ahead. I'll be along soon enough."

Percy slapped the reins, and the wagon moved on, going west.

When they were out of sight, Malachi and the Captain looked at each other and laughed.

"Home, Malachi, we're goin' home. Think of it. Home! I never thought I'd live to see the day. For us, the war is over." Malory said, placing his hands on Malachi's shoulders. "Well, are ya ready? Let's go."

"I'm not goin' with ya, Captain."

A confused look washed over the captain's face.

"What are ya sayin'?"

"Just what I said, I ain't goin'. I'm staying here."

Malory took his hands off Malachi's shoulder and backed away.

"Here? What's here?"

"My life," Malachi said softly. "I found me a place in this world, and I'm gonna live it. These are good people, and I need them even more than they need me. And I love the Lord, and I love workin' for him. Besides all that, I got a young boy relying on me; and I ain't gonna let him down."

Malory smiled and shook his head. "Well, I never..." He reached out and shook Malachi's hand. "Ya take care of yourself. Ya hear me?"

Malachi just smiled. He reached into his coat pocket, pulled out an envelope, and handed it to the captain.

"Do me a favor," said Malachi. "When this is all over and the dust has settled, get this to my mother."

Malory took the envelope, folded it, and placed it in his top pocket.

When they both came to the realization there was nothing more to say, Captain Malory turned and started down the road heading east. He resisted the urge to look back one more time and wave. And in a moment, he was out of view.

Malachi stood in the middle of the road. The night wind, cool, blew into his face, pushing his hair back. He could hear the commotion going on at the compound. It was time to leave. He turned to the west and began walking. Before he got more than ten feet, he heard a voice in the darkness.

"You've done a man's job," said the voice.

"Who said that?" Malachi asked.

The figure of a man stepped out from behind a tree.

"I ain't surprised at how well ya done. But what I think is important is how surprised ya are at yourself."

The man stepped forward to make himself known.

"Marcellus!" shouted Malachi, smiling from ear to ear. "I can't believe my eyes. What are ya doin' here?"

"Lettin' the Spirit take me where he wants me to go, preachin' the Good Word."

Malachi looked him up and down.

"Ya look good, Marcellus. I see ya got a new preacher's suit."

"Yeah, that be the easy part. As ya well know by now, the clothes don't really make the man. It's what he does that matters."

"I can't thank ya enough," said Malachi. "You've given me so much."

"I ain't given ya nothin' that ya didn't already have. The Lord gives everybody a gift. It's a blessed man who gets to find out what it is and live it out."

Marcellus reached out; the two men shook hands. But somehow that didn't seem like enough. Malachi lunged forward and the two hugged each other. After a moment, Marcellus gently broke the hold and took a few steps away.

"Marcellus, where are ya goin'? I got a church now. I'd be honored if ya come with me and see it. Maybe visit for a few weeks."

"I've already seen it," Marcellus said. "And a fine church it is. I got to talk to some of the folks, and they had nothin' but good things to say about their pastor. And that boy, Emmanuel, he loves ya, too. He told me so himself."

"He did?" Malachi asked.

"Well, not in so many words. But I know he does."

"Will I ever see ya again?"

"Listen to ya, talkin' like a man with no faith. Of course we'll see each other again, if not in this world then in the next. But as for this world, it wouldn't surprise me if the Spirit moved me through these parts again someday."

Malachi reached out and hugged the old man again. Then Marcellus smiled, turned, and started down the road heading east.

As he walked out of view, Malachi could hear him singing.

I must walk my lonesome valley
I got to walk it for myself

Nobody else can walk it for me
I got to walk it for myself

I must go and stand my trial
I got to stand it for myself

A Slave's Song

Nobody else can stand it for me
I got to stand it for myself

Jesus walked his lonesome valley
He had to walk it for himself

Nobody else could walk it for him
He had to walk it for himself

There was a golden hue coming over the crest of the eastern horizon. The sun was coming up. Malachi turned and started walking westward. If he hurried, he'd be back in time to make breakfast for Emmanuel.

THE END

Michael Edwin Q. is available for book interviews and personal appearances. For more information contact:

Michael Edwin Q.
C/O Advantage Books
P.O. Box 160847
Altamonte Springs, FL 32716
michaeledwinq.com

Other Titles in this series by Michael Edwin Q:

Born A Colored Girl: 978-1-59755-478-4
Pappy Moses' Peanut Plantation: 978-1-59755-482-8
But Have Not Love: 978-1-59755-494-7
Tame the Savage Heart: 978-1-59755-5098

To purchase additional copies of these book visit our bookstore website at:
www.advbookstore.com

Longwood, Florida, USA
"we bring dreams to life" ™
www.advbookstore.com

CPSIA information can be obtained
at www.ICGtesting.com
Printed in the USA
BVHW081933160619
551141BV00002B/497/P